THE COMING OF G-7

"Arrived at tertiary planet, minor star, parsec 11.6, axis 86.36. Survey reveals ambulatory organisms. Am stationed for investment.

G-7

Here, where horses clip-clopped beside a murmuring river, where insects hummed from the roadsides, there was little need for alertness and less for wariness. Had he seen it, the driver would have paid no heed to a boulder jutting from a precipice five hundred yards ahead where the road swung sharply through a narrow defile cut by the Snake. Above the stagecoach, the eagle continued to circle, watching the movements of the horses with a predator's curiosity, but the eagle was not the sole observer of the man and horses.

Atop the crest, the boulder was also watching.

Andromeda Gun
John Boyd

A BERKLEY MEDALLION BOOK
published by
BERKLEY PUBLISHING CORPORATION

Copyright © 1974, by Boyd Upchurch

All rights reserved

Published by arrangement with Charles Neighbors, Inc.

All rights reserved which includes the right to reproduce this book or portions thereof in any form whatsoever. For information address

Charles Neighbors, Inc.
240 Waverly Place
New York, New York 10014

Library of Congress Catalog Card Number: 74-79640

SBN 425-02878-X

BERKLEY MEDALLION BOOKS are published by
Berkley Publishing Corporation
200 Madison Avenue
New York, N. Y. 10016

BERKLEY MEDALLION BOOK ® TM 757,375

Printed in the United States of America

Berkley Medallion Edition, JULY, 1975

1

FOR eons, as men measure time, the species had watched the dying of its light, the slow waning of its planet's sun, and by the then-immutable Second Law of Thermodynamics the race was doomed by entropy.

But it was not a breed to go gently into its long night. Once its sons and daughters had stridden long-limbed through the planet's morning (though that was long, long ago, and to move limbs required calories), so memory helped spur the race to find means of conserving energy. Through the darkness and pale daylights of its dying planet, it strove to prevent its own extinction, to revoke the Second Law.

The race had succeeded.

Now there were no longer sons and daughters, no organic heirs, only the race, lambent and protean, ethereal and far-ranging, the race immortal, for it had discovered the secrets of light. More, it had found the abstract and eternal Truth of Light.

It had come to its truth in steps, solving problems that begat problems. With its planet's petrochemicals exhausted, with lumens falling weakly through the freezing air, the organic progenitors of the penultimate species brought heat and light to the twilit globe through the introduction of hydrogen fusion, but the hydrogen consumed in the process was necessary for the organisms' existence. Thus all solutions led only to the ultimate problem and a final solution as awesome in its implications as it was in its technological challenge.

Seek, find, and re-create the anatomy of the angel.

The solution: Remove the electron from the hydrogen nucleus, retaining only the plasma; encapsulate a maximum of plasma in a minimal organism through the electrolysis of an organic embryo. Once the circulatory pattern of the plasma is established by the embryo's arterial system, place the embryo in a tachyon incubator and bombard the plasma, shattering the hydrogen nuclei into photons. After the photons are established as a circulatory light system by the arterial patterns of the embryo, atrophy the organism and disembody the light.

By trial and fewer and fewer errors, light was integrated and homogenized around a fusion-fission core. In the ultimate synthesis of energy and matter, after the organism withered away, only photons, the essence of pure being, remained. Swirling in the self-directed patterns men call intelligence, they wafted themselves through the darkening air or hung pendulous over the crested palls of their grand family funerals.

Selfless, immortal—and ineffectual—the ineffable descendants of organic forebears were form without substance, ardor without hormones, wills without power, but it had been foreseen that the limbo in which the beings existed would offend their inherited logic and affront the valor of a race which had not ceased from mortal fight until all else was overcome, even time which proved a part of the mysteries of light.

So the luminosities needed electrochemical organisms to invest and direct. They needed host beings with levered limbs and opposing thumbs to convert the wisdom of their race into good works. Still sentient, still unsatisfied, impelled by racial memories of an olden time entombed, the beings would never have been content to function as diffused light triggering random packets of chlorophyll, nor as focused light for casual illuminations, and certainly not as coherent light which can rend and destroy. Offspring of a forcible breed, they little cared to waver as pale violet light over the ruins of a dying planet. Instead, they would bring order to the energy in the bright corners of their galaxy. They would spread their wisdom to the sun-fed planets of other star clusters. With borrowed senses they would know again music and bright-eyed loves, with borrowed fingers build again their sunny domes of rare device.

These purposes, too, had been foreseen when the progenitors of the nebulosities earlier constructed miniaturized, single-entity starships with photoelectric guidance systems. By imparting speed, range and directional controls unavailable to the unassisted beings, the vehicles were designed to waft the angels on their flights across interstellar distances. Trundling up from the interior of the planet on automated assembly lines, the starships were moved onto launching pads. There the pilots angeled the craft and lifted off with the sound of tearing silk, plashing the long-dimmed skies with the spurn of their wakes.

Over the margins of the worlds they sped and fretted the far-flung boundaries of the stars, interlacing nebulae with the skeins of ultra-ultra-high-frequency communication. They found and invested host organisms through which the heritage of their race might survive and through which matter might be woven into richer tapestries of life. On the planets they visited, they brought long peace to cornland, alp, and sea.

But theirs was not a unilateral giving.

Once more they were able to feel the warmth of sunlight on cheeks or jowls. They reexperienced the homely joys of organic existence: the gut-expanding repletion of food and its tense tendoned release; fresh awakenings from the sweet satiety of sleep; dew smells at morning and starshine at night. They heard music and birdsong, flowing water and rushing wind. They relearned laughter quickly, for they held to the detachment from which humor springs. Being immortal, they felt with recurring delight the pangs of young love on the principally bisexual planets they inhabited. On the unisexual planets they knew the thrill of self-pollination; on polysexual planets the more diffused joy of group encounters. But the luminosities found their most abiding joy in work performed.

Rechanneling energies, they brought order from organic chaos. Often they invested brutish organisms whose behavior they reformed into patterns men call sainthood. The scouts brought species after species into the Galactic Brotherhood, species which varied from the gentle fahlahs of Doremia, themselves so nebulous they barely cast shadows, to the stalkthorns of Mirfak who pollinated by dagger thrusts. When they went forth to battle, they always won.

Until the Light Bearers encountered Man.

While, with unhurried haste and unperturbed pace, the luminosities had spread over and encompassed the Milky Way, and inexplicable disaster was recorded in a message flashed across the spaceways:

ONE OF OUR PROBES IS MISSING!

The message was sent through the galaxies on the third survey of the wheel galaxy the Brotherhood designated M-17. In part, it was a tribute to Central Intelligence, in greater part a tribute to the scouts, that only one expedition vanished, because dangers did exist for the scouts. There were dark holes in space, neutron stars whose tremendous gravitational pull sucked in light quanta, and there was the danger of a loss of entropy in luminosities trapped, by some means, on cul-de-sac planets.

Officially the file was closed on Galactic Probe Three. Mathematics almost precluded a solution to the disappearance, for there were many stars in the nebula and many, many planets. More probes came as M-17 wheeled through the void, and always, when they neared the coordinates where G-3 vanished, the probes brought wonderment with them. Among scouts of the Galactic Brotherhood's Interplanetary Exploration Legion, the loss was never forgotten.

Still, two millennia later, no hint of a second catastrophe was contained in the preliminary report received at Galactic Central in M-17 from the seventh scout sent into the sector:

> Arrived at tertiary planet, minor star, parsec 11.6, axis 86.36. Survey reveals ambulatory organisms. Am stationed for investment.
>
> G-7

Aloft, an eagle soared in the afternoon sunlight, tipping its wings to updrafts from the Grand Teton. Drowsing atop the Territorial Stage Lines stagecoach, the driver felt no impulse to look upward as his horses plodded beside the Snake River, untended in their final five-mile pull toward Shoshone Flats. August heat, the sway of the stagecoach, and the creak of harness leather added to the driver's somnolence.

Here where horses clip-clopped beside a murmuring river, where insects hummed from the roadsides, there was little need for alertness and less for wariness. Had he seen it, the driver would have paid no heed to a boulder jutting from a precipice five hundred yards ahead where the road swung sharply through a narrow defile cut by the Snake. Above the stagecoach, the eagle continued to circle, watching the movements of the horses with a predator's curiosity, but the eagle was not the sole observer of the man and horses.

Atop the crest, the boulder was also watching.

Inside the naturally camouflaged space vehicle, impressions received not solely from light but from more subtle emanations recorded the structure of the vehicle below, the texture of the leather, the grain of the wood, heat and heat variations. Sensors weighed the moisture content of breath, traced coursing blood, sought and found electrical impulses in brains.

Within the metering segment of the spaceship, the scout scanned the encephalogram of the driver, then passed swiftly over the brain readings of the horses and those of a passenger inside the coach whose beta waves registered but faintly. Minute adjustments occurred in the crystals of the space rock when the electromagnetic warp created by the driver's bone structure revealed flexible digits on his hand and a musculature that permitted opposing motion in one of the digits. All meterings ceased, their object accomplished; G-7 had discovered the ultimate index of an organism's capabilities, the driver's thumb.

The erect quadrupled, the one with the synchronous brain waves in an activated cerebral cortex, was a suitable host. G-7 sent an action report to Galactic Central: "Am investing host organism."

G-7 flowed into the diffusion chamber, expanded its light content below the level of visibility, and emerged from the spaceship. For a moment it hovered over the spaceship, testing for an absence of shadow and waiting for the stagecoach to pass beneath it. Its luminosity was lost in the sunlight. It cast no shadow. Ahead of the stagecoach, it sensed a sharp bend where the road almost overhung the river curving below.

Then, gliding along the magnetic force lines of earth, G-7 zoomed toward the horses.

With the curve in the road twenty yards ahead, G-7 dipped low over the heads of the beasts and shrilled, electronically, a note too high for the driver to detect against the tympanums of the horses' ears. Maddened by pain, the beasts bolted. The stage lurched forward, gaining speed despite the reining of the aroused driver. Flayed by the keening of G-7, the horses thundered onto the curve, swinging around it, but the stage had become a juggernaut not to be diverted.

It swayed and keeled too far, swinging out over the embankment, and toppled, cartwheeling twice before it smashed to a halt so close to the river that its remaining right wheel continued to spin over the water's edge. Both trailing horses had been dragged off the road with the stagecoach, but the leading span, saved by a broken center pole, trotted to a halt down the road, trailing their severed harnesses, as G-7's keening dwindled into silence.

G-7 hovered over the wreckage, personally metering the

close-in data. It had not intended to destroy, but, obviously, the organisms offered poor survival capabilities. One of the quadrupeds had been pierced by the broken center pole, which had barely penetrated its arterial pump, but the pump was malfunctioning in a drastic manner. One lay immobilized by a simple fracture of a single limb.

Far more important to G-7, the erect quadruped with the levered thumb had been thrown from the seat with sufficient force to snap the column supporting its brain housing, and it was emitting no neural impulses at all.

G-7's selected host, the driver, had ceased to function.

Inside the stage, the passenger was functioning with no additional impairments to its nerve or brain structure. In fact, the organism had failed to awaken at the crash. From previous meterings, G-7 had rejected the passenger as a host, would have, in fact, preferred the horses had it not been for the sleeper's thumb.

G-7 drifted through the underside of the stagecoach and entered the skull pan of the sleeper, tapping the energy of its thalamus, sending tracers out to explore the sleeper's memory, language, and knowledge.

It sensed potentialities in the brain mechanism. In fact, the brain was made up almost entirely of potentialities, all unrealized. Memories traced along the whorls and loops of neurons connected visions of warfare, death, and violence. G-7 followed a history that led from the battlefields of northern Virginia to gunfights in a place called Texas and across a river into a place called Mexico, to friendship with a Mexican, Hey You Garcia, and to numberless brawls in cantinas. But all memories led to a moonswept desert in Utah where a man called Colonel Blicket laughed above smoking guns which had killed Garcia and mouthed a foul insult to the absent owner of the mind G-7 occupied, Johnny Loco.

The vileness of the epithet spoken by the colonel was so revolting to the sleeper that the words were blocked by the subconscious machinery of the being who called himself a man, but even the blocked memory caused such discords in the brain that G-7 quickly shunted its explorations to less-disturbed areas.

Vastnesses of untapped energy lay in the brain pod, and the untapped areas were neutral, neither good nor evil. If this organism were to become the instrument by which its species would be led to galactic brotherhood, then molecular patterns would have to be reoriented and unused neurons activated. What little potential toward goodness the man had developed was so far gone into darkness that even his name was shrouded. The man who called himself Johnny Loco had been born Ian McCloud.

First, he would have to be guided into cooperation with his species, for in his own language the man was an outlaw, a term which implied some law he was outside of. Tracing the concept of "law" through the brain's conceptual areas, G-7 arrived at: going to church; keeping cleaned and shaved; being polite to women; not robbing and killing.

Probing tentacles of light diverged through the sleeper's brain, connecting synapses, jury-rigging junctions between the man's atrophied love centers and his equally disused concepts of social responsibility. G-7 was making its first attempt to guide the man, prompting him to take his first step in which appeared to be a journey of a thousand miles toward respectability.

Now interwoven with the neuron patterns of its host, using the man's language, G-7 felt its first human emotion. It thrilled to the knowledge that this currently saddleless saddle tramp, this ignoble brute it had inhabited, would eventually be hailed by others of its species as Saint Ian the First.

At the moment, storms sweeping from the vagus nerve were battering the man's thalamus. Nudging a neuron here, straightening a chain of molecules there, G-7 went about pacifying the brain's outraged stomach as Johnny Loco stirred, stretched, and opened his eyes.

G-7 was amazed by the clarity, range, the depth and color perception of the man's binocular vision. At the angle at which he lay, the man could see the crest of the defile, and from five hundred yards G-7 could estimate the cubic volume of the boulder atop the crest, the spaceship which had brought it to this planet called earth in a galaxy called the Milky Way from a star cluster which, it would later learn, men had named Andromeda.

Drifting into full wakefulness, Johnny Loco noticed first his boots on the seat above his head with his feet still in them. He could not recall when he had last slept with his feet over his head, but it was a good position for curing a hangover. Ordinarily he would have been very sick from the rotgut he had drunk last night in Idaho Falls.

Idaho Falls! The very words rang as a knell, and he closed his eyes again to shut out his memories. He had bet a hundred dollars on a two-card draw to an inside straight and had lost the pot to a pair of jacks. He had bet and lost his horse and saddle and had tried to bet his pistol, but the other gamblers would not let him bet the weapon. It had a hair trigger, and its handle was so full of notches that drawing it was like grabbing a saw.

If he couldn't learn to play poker, he might as well quit robbing banks, he thought. All he had left from the Boise holdup was thirty-seven cents and a ticket to Shoshone Flats, Wyoming Territory. Remembering the stage ticket, he could account for the position of his boots. The stagecoach had overturned, which meant he had paid good money for fare to nowhere, and if he didn't make Shoshone Flats by six the bank would be closed. He reopened his eyes, suddenly alert.

Today was Saturday and if he didn't get to the bank before closing time, he'd have no funds for Sunday. It was against his principles to rob banks after hours or after dark. He was a bank robber, not a night-crawling burglar, so it was imperative that he get to town in time to find and steal a fast horse for his getaway and rob the bank before nightfall. Still marveling at his clear head and unroiled stomach, he climbed through the window and looked over the wreckage.

One glance at the angle of the driver's head told him the man's neck was broken. One of the horses was dead, and the other, still in harness, had a broken foreleg. Loco slid down from the side of the stagecoach, walked over, pulled his pistol, and killed the lame horse in an act of mercy so conventional it was unaccompanied by compassion for the beast. Reloading and reholstering his pistol, he knelt beside the body of the driver and pulled the man's wallet from his pocket. He riffled through the contents.

There was a paper dollar and a two-dollar meal ticket with eighty cents unpunched drawn on a Miss Stewart's Restaurant in Shoshone Flats. The ticket was made out to Will Trotter by the Territorial Stage Lines. Loco kept the dollar and returned the meal ticket to the wallet when he noticed the width of the dead man's belt. He unbuckled the belt and slid it out of the belt straps.

Apparently Will Trotter had not been a trusting person. Loco found nine silver dollars concealed in the belt. That sum, with an additional twenty-three cents he found in the driver's jeans was the extent of his salvage. Loco was not disappointed. He had robbed banks for less money.

Standing, he looked up at the road and saw the two lead horses farther down munching on the roadside grass. He climbed the hill and walked down the road to take the reins of the first horse, a Percheron. It was no horse for a man of his calling, but it was as good as the Clydesdale farther down the road, good enough to carry him within stealing distance of a faster horse. He started to swing aboard the Percheron when, for the first time in his life, Johnny Loco reconsidered.

Here was an opportunity to become respectable. If he took Will Trotter's body into Shoshone Flats, he would be regarded as a citizen doing his duty. He was twenty-eight, time for him to start thinking about making his old age a possibility. He couldn't go on forever as an itinerant bank robber.

He held the idea at arm's length, eyeing it distastefully. Respectability was for women and men with green eyeshades and bankers who put mortgages on the homes of widows and orphans. Admittedly he wasn't called Johnny Loco without a reason, but he had not yet gone plumb loco.

Yet the idea had its good points. Neither of these heavy draft horses could get him close enough to town and leave him much time to spare for finding a faster horse, stealing it, and robbing the bank. If he rode in on an errand of mercy, bringing Will Trotter's corpse, his behavior might lull the natural suspicion of the natives toward a stranger and give him more time to act unobserved. He could spend a leisurely half hour or so finding a fast horse, steal it, rob the bank, and pound leather to Green River where he would bushwhack Colonel Blicket and the sergeant.

Suddenly he realized he was planning ahead. Colonel Blicket had always been a great one for plans. Maybe the master's lessons were finally getting through to the student, Loco thought, as he walked down the road and grasped the head harness of the Percheron.

The beast balked at a stranger's touch, swerving its head away from the man. With a beautiful demonstration of brute power and fearlessness, in G-7's opinion, the man jerked the horse's head around, slapped its jaw with a resounding whack, and said curtly, "Move, you son of a bitch!"

In utter obeisance, with complete docility, the great beast moved to follow the man. Shades of the stalkthorns of Mirfak! But the man had commanded with the flat of his hand.

Back at the body, Loco, augmenting his plan to appear honest, put eleven cents back into the dead man's trouser pockets and buckled the dead man's money belt back on while G-7 made an instantaneous reevaluation of the host it had occupied. The brute beauty and valor here buckling contained too much energy to be controlled outright without a loss of fissioning power. Its host would have to be nudged or enticed toward the light, and at the moment its most likely lure seemed to be this mysterious Colonel Blicket whose insult had aroused in its host such implacable hatred. Hatred, G-7 realized, was a negative motivational force, but it could find no positive forces in the brain of its host nearly so strong.

Very well, G-7 decided, let hatred be the spur to raise this ignoble spirit.

Unaware that his fate was being decided, Johnny Loco draped the one-hundred-and-seventy pound body over the Percheron with casual ease and said aloud to himself, "Yeah, I either got to learn to play poker or quit robbing banks, unless I can find some richer banks to rob."

Again the man was unaware that the addition of the last phrase to his sentence had catapulted him to heights of intelligence he had never before achieved. Always in the past his thinking had been "either-or." Now he had added an option, and he weighed the option. After he robbed the bank at Shoshone Flats and killed the colonel at Green River, he might head east and hold up the more prosperous banks back in the States.

The being inside was acutely aware that Ian McCloud—it rejected the alias as untruthful—was perverting its suggestion that he carry the body into town. The man did not regard his proposed actions as a step toward respectability but as a ruse for facilitating the theft of a horse. Still G-7 was not dismayed. Old habit patterns, it knew, often persisted, but it also knew that time, the implacable foe of large-molecule organisms, was on its side. Day and night the silent hammers of reformation would be pounding in this man's brain.

Meanwhile G-7 had more pleasant observations to make, more pertinent data to absorb about this planet men called earth.

Golden light from a young sun fell lavishly on this side of the globe, warming the cheeks of the man and triggering universal photosynthesis in lush grass across the floor of a valley dotted with herds of cattle and spotted, here and there, with fenced fields of hay and corn. Northwestward the peaks of the mountains soared to snow-tipped summits. Forests of stately trees skirted the lower fringes of the peaks. It was a many-shaded world of blues, greens, whites, grays, varicolored flowers, and, toward the south, the silver sheen of the river seen through a lacework of pale green cottonwoods and willows. The pure air held enough hydrogen to fuel untold fusion furnaces for millennia, and once, when the man forded a creek and stopped to drink, G-7 found the water cool and pure in its native state.

The man, possessing limited but acute senses, was the only discord in this symphonic flow of free energy. Riding slouched on the broad back of the horse, he needed but to inhale and his nose registered and clarified the syrupy redolence of alfalfa, the lushness of grass, the pungency of pine resin, the musky maleness of corn pollen. His ears recorded the roadside scurryings of chipmunks, identified insect sounds, the thump of a falling pinecone in the woods to his left, and, far to southward, the plaintive lowing of a cow. Yet this rich panoply of sounds and smells was keyed on a strange alertness. McCloud was sniffing the air for human body odor, listening for the metallic click of a rifle's bolt. Though seemingly indolent and relaxed, the man rode in wariness of his fellow human beings.

G-7 was no stranger to violence, but interspecies destructiveness ordinarily occurred from collisions on crowded planets. Here, where no other human being or human habitation was visible for miles, McCloud feared for his life, and he only feared for it because he wanted to live long enough to kill Colonel Blicket and his aide-de-camp.

This was a world of paradoxes mystifying even to a universal intelligence. A bank robber who risked his life for the possession of material trinkets lived to avenge an insult, a nonmaterial epithet. Obviously McCloud's pride had been offended by the colonel's abusive language, and pride was a cardinal sin. Very well, G-7 decided, it would use the man's sin, tempt him with dishonest trifles to betray him into righteous consequences.

Three hours of sunlight were left—the bank would still be open—when Ian McCloud rode into the outskirts of Shoshone Flats with Will Trotter's body draped over the trailing horse. He felt ill at east as he approached the two rows of sod shanties, log huts, and frame buildings strung along the wagon ruts of the main street. Leading a funeral cortege into a strange town was a job for an undertaker's assistant; the production of corpses, not their processing, was his line of business.

Frame buildings grew more frequent as he approached the midsection of the town. Looking over the horses he saw tethered or before hitching racks, he could not see one more suited to running than to pulling a plow. Most of the beasts looked winded while standing still, those that were able to stand, and the Clydesdale he rode would have been even money against most of them in a race.

An old lady in a sunbonnet, holding the hand of a boy of ten or so, was the first citizen he saw. She stood at the frayed beginnings of a boardwalk, leaning over and peering at the body on the horse behind him as he rode up.

Politely tipping his hat, he asked, "Ma'm, who's sheriff of this here town?"

"Sheriff Faust. . . . Run ahead, Hickam, and wake the old gentleman up. . . . Land sakes, young man, is that Will Trotter you got there?"

"Yes'm," he answered, as the boy turned and ran down the sidewalk. "I reckon it was."

"Lordy mercy," she exclaimed, falling into stride with the Percheron, "this is going to break Trudy Spence's heart. Him and her been engaged for three years. Poor Trudy! Widowed afore she's wed . . . Dead Man's Curve got him. Am I right, young man?"

"Yes'm. I reckon."

"I knowed it. You can't fool Betsy Troop about that road. Been traveling it for twenty years. Traveled it afore the Indians moved out and the Mormons moved in. Don't know which of them two I'd rather have. Either one would outrun the other in a two-man race to the boondocks. . . . Well, I'll say this for Will Trotter, he looks natural, except his head's kinda on backwards. . . . You can't fool me about Dead Man's Curve, mister. Only time that curve's safe for vehicles is when there's forty two feet of snow on the road. People around here won't do nothing about it either. Reckon they figure if they wait long enough, that kink's going to grow out of the road."

Betsy Troop's monologue, begun for McCloud as a chatty conversation, swelled to a tirade directed against a growing audience as more wayside idlers fell into step with the ambling Percheron, commenting on its burden with low voices.

"Can't expect them Mormons to do no road work, what with them planting all day and plowing all night. . . ."

McCloud rode on, aloof above the tumult, as Betsy Troop, having dismissed the Mormons, turned her attention to "the lazy, no-count Gentiles" gathering alongside the Percheron. He directed the cortege toward the sheriff's office, recognizable from the barred windows at the rear of the stone building, and pulled up before the front porch. A tall, gray-haired man emerged, tugging a suspender over a shoulder, his star pinned to the top half of a suit of gray flannel underwear. He had the dignity of age if not the authority in his manner as he walked down from the porch to look at the body.

The crowd grew silent, waiting for the sheriff to speak, and in the pause Ian McCloud had time to decipher the sign posted on the front of the building:

CITIZENS: PLEASE DO NOT DISCHARGE FIRE-ARMS INSIDE THE TOWN LIMITS. . . . SHERIFF FAUST

Sheriff Faust cleared his throat and said, "I'll be, if it ain't Will Trotter. Dead Man's Curve get him, son?"

"Yes, sir."

"Then he died outside my jurisdiction. Why didn't you leave him there? Buzzards wouldn't bother him, not for a couple of hours anyhow. Let the stage line go bring him in."

"I thought it was my Christian duty, sir."

"Reckon you would think that"—the sheriff nodded—"not being familiar with the Territorial Stage Lines. I suspect the town owes you a vote of thanks anyway. What's your name?"

He started to answer, "Johnny Loco," and paused. Chances

15

were, the sheriff would be more apt to recognize his alias than his name.

"Ian McCloud," he answered, and the name sounded strange on his lips.

"The town thanks you, Mr. McCloud. Now, would you haul Will three buildings down to the Territorial Stage Lines' office and let Mr. Birnie, the stationmaster, take care of the matter."

Yawning slightly, the sheriff turned and went back into the jail, apparently to resume his afternoon nap. McCloud glanced at the horse tied to the jailhouse hitching rack. The sheriff's nag wasn't worth stealing. He nudged the draft horses forward.

Mr. Birnie, the stationmaster, was summoned from an early supper by someone in the crowd. Judging by the girth of the man who waddled from the door, McCloud figured it to be the first of a bunch of suppers. Birnie's shirt was unbuttoned above the belt because the lower buttonholes couldn't reach the buttons, and his belt, looped below his protruding navel, was as much a hammock for his belly as a support for his trousers. The stationmaster was munching on a half-moon pie as he walked onto the porch.

McCloud explained the circumstances of Trotter's death and returned the dead man's wallet, publicly itemizing its contents.

Birnie took the wallet, finished his pie, and declaimed to the crowd in a petulant whine, "Now, this beats all get-out. Long as that galoot's been driving this run, he goes and wrecks my stagecoach. Haul him down to Near-Sighted Charlie's, mister. Charlie's the undertaker. Tell him I'll be down later to settle the estate."

McCloud bridled at the order. "Mister Birnie, I done my Christian duty, getting this poor soul to where he was paid to get me. You can take him from here. But I had a ticket to Green River which was lost with all my clothes and money when my valise fell in the river."

"How much money you lose?"

"Better than eighty dollars."

"I can sure sympathize with your loss, Mr. McCloud, because I just lost a six-hundred-and-fifty-dollar stagecoach. Between you and me, I figure I'm about five-hundred-and-seventy dollars more deserving of sympathy."

Ian knew from the man's plaintive voice he would get no rebate on his nonexistent clothes and money, but there was the possibility he might be refunded for the imaginary ticket to Green River.

"I sympathize with you, Mr. Birnie, but I wasn't under no contract to get your stagecoach to Shoshone Flats. You sold me contract to get me to Green River. Since I ain't getting there, I think you ought to give me my money back."

"Where'd you buy your ticket?"

"Pocatello."

"Mr. McCloud, I can't give you money that's back in Pocatello, but I'll play fair with you. We got another stage coming through, Tuesday. You can ride it, free of charge, if the durned driver can get it around Dead Man's Curve."

"Tuesday!" Ian exploded. "You mean I got to set here till Tuesday, with all my money and clothes floating down the river. How'm I going to eat and sleep till Tuesday?"

"Times is hard, son"—Birnie shook his head dolefully—"but I ain't no innkeeper. I run a stage line."

"Least you can do is give me the driver's meal ticket. He ain't going to use it."

"Son, that's the company's meal ticket."

"Give him the meal ticket, Birnie"—a tall, red-haired man shouldered his way through the crowd—"or, so help me, if I catch you eating on that ticket at Miss Stewart's, you're going to lose about three hundred of them five hundred pounds before you get off the stool."

Birnie flinched at the big man's anger and reconsidered his position. "Well, seeing as how you brought in the horses, Mr. McCloud, I reckon the company can afford to be generous. Here's the meal ticket."

As Birnie handed up the meal ticket to McCloud, still astride the horse, the tall man turned and said, "My name's Bain, Mr. McCloud. You can take the ticket to Miss Stewart's. Her place is right across from my saloon. As far as your sleeping arrangements are concerned, you can hole up, upstairs over my barroom, till Tuesday, if you don't mind a little female company."

"No, Mr. Bain," a man called from an outer circle of the crowd, "he can have the choice room at my hotel till Tuesday. He did his Christian duty by Brother Trotter and I'll do my Christian duty by him. If that meal ticket runs out before Tuesday, son, you tell Miss Stewart to charge your meals to Jack Taylor."

Ian appreciated all that was being done for him as he used his last few seconds atop the Clydesdale to survey the horses up and down the street. From where he sat, he could not see a horse he judged capable of outrunning a Tennessee walker. Still, all the palaver going on around him was about nothing. He'd take their meals and room, if he had to, and stay long enough to find a decent horse, but, come Monday, he'd ride out of here with all their money, heading for Green River and Colonel Blicket.

Followed by admiring looks from the crowd, he slid from the horse and angled across the street toward Miss Stewart's Restaurant.

So it was that Ian McCloud, alias Johnny Loco, coming in part from the defeated armies of Robert E. Lee and in part from the great nebula in Andromeda, arrived in Shoshone Flats, Wyoming Territory. The stride carrying him across the wagon ruts was given additional jauntiness by the success of his plan, so far, to rob a bank and murder a colonel and by the first stirrings, deep in the nodes of his brain, of a drive toward sainthood.

Of saintliness Ian knew little, only a remembered aphorism dragged laboriously from McGuffey's Third Reader that virtue had its own rewards. Awaiting him at the restaurant was the second lesson: that virtue could be as parsimonious as the Territorial Stage Lines. Inwardly the nobler being now diffused along the neuron paths of McCloud contemplated with keener awareness a different observation: In this small cluster of the breed called "man" it had observed pride, avarice, anger, gluttony, envy, and sloth—six of the seven deadly sins.

Awaiting it in the restaurant was the seventh, lust.

2

SUNLIGHT through a western window fell on the golden hair of a waitress, sole occupant of Miss Stewart's Restaurant, who stood behind the counter reading a book with such intentness that she did not look up until Ian was seated on a stool across from her. When she lifted her head and he caught her eyes, cool yet friendly, their blueness accented by a swash of freckles beneath them, he took off his hat.

"Ma'am, I got a meal ticket from the stage lines that belonged to Will Trotter, deceased. If Miss Stewart should question you. . . ."

"I'm Miss Stewart," she said, moving down the counter and leaning slightly over it to smile toward him, "Miss Gabriella Stewart. I saw you bringing in Brother Trotter's body, so you must be Mr. Ian McCloud."

"Yes'm," he said. He had placed her age at eighteen, but she had to be older if she owned the restaurant and read books. He wondered how she had learned his name so quickly, since she had not been among the spectators gathered to see the body. "Hope I didn't turn your customers' stomachs, hauling a dead man past your window. I must have been a sight."

"Oh, no, sir," she assured him as she handed him a menu. " 'I wad some power the giftie gie us,' as Sir Walter Scott says, so you could have seen yourself riding into our town as a Sir Galahad on a draft horse bearing Brother Trotter like the Holy Grail. Brother Trotter was respected among us Methodists. He was a deacon of our church."

She had taken a peculiar stance to deliver her benediction, backing toward the front window as she spoke and leaning across the counter, as if she were shielding her face from a view from the street.

Without looking at it, he laid the menu down. "I'd like steak and potatoes, ma'am."

"Mr. McCloud, I can't recommend my steak this week. It's a little gristly. But my fried chicken is the best you ever tasted."

He glanced at the book she had laid on the counter and said, "All right, Miss Stewart. I'll take fried chicken and potatoes."

He could decipher the word "Bacon" on the front of the book. Assuming it was a cookbook, he said politely, "I'd like to compliment you on your choice of reading matter, ma'am. Ain't many young ladies who'd be reading up on their work while they're working."

"Yes," she agreed, putting a place setting in front of him, "but I have to sharpen my mind for my children."

She wore no wedding band, so her remark interested him.

"How many young ones you got, ma'am?"

"Fourteen, but I'd have more if I could get help from the Mormons in this valley."

His soaring expectations suddenly fell as he realized she was a schoolteacher. That accounted for the children, the book and the "Miss" everybody put in front of her name.

"Ma'am, I'd think every man in this valley would be glad to do anything you wanted."

"The lower half of the valley is all Mormons," she said. "They won't put their children in a Gentile school. Mr. Bryce Peyton, the stake superintendent, says he doesn't want to get his angels mixed up with our angels."

"Still, you must be busy with fourteen, teaching them and running a restaurant."

"My mother helps during schooltime. Pa used to run the restaurant, but he was killed this spring in a fall from a horse."

Her cooking range, set back in an alcove, was within talking distance of his stool. He watched as she bent to put in more firewood and turned to slice his potatoes. All schoolteachers had high ideals, he knew, but this girl had something more—lean flanks, well-turned shanks, and the prettiest haunch he had seen north of Sonora.

Schoolteachers went to respectable places, he reflected, like church, and a church hitching rack would be a good place from which to steal a fast horse. Ranchers would be riding their best animals to church, and the preacher would keep them occupied for at least an hour while the beasts went unguarded. Schoolteachers were seen only with respectable men, but, temporarily, Ian McCloud was a respectable man.

"Are you open Sundays, ma'am?"

"No, I'm not, Mr. McCloud, but I could fix you a box of chicken good for three meals, tomorrow, for the amount you'll have left on Brother Trotter's meal ticket."

"I might take you up on that. Is there a Methodist church hereabouts?"

"Why, yes, Mr. McCloud." Her face within the alcove flashed him a smile. "It's just south of town. Brother Winchester preaches a fine sermon. Tomorrow, he's going to tell us about heaven. If you care to join us, I'd be pleased to sit next to you and introduce you to our congregation."

"If you're willing to be so kind, Miss Stewart, I'd be happy to hire a rig and carry you to church."

"I'd be honored to let you, Mr. McCloud, but I'm spoke for, coming and going. It's only after I get there that I'm alone."

"Reckon I should have figured that, Miss Stewart. A girl as pretty as you would be sure to have a courter for going and one for coming."

"No, Mr. McCloud. Billy Peyton's my only suitor. But he's a Mormon and won't go in. He just waits outside."

Her remark dismayed him. It would be harder to steal a horse with Billy Peyton waiting outside the church. "If Peyton's willing to court you, seems to me he'd be willing to take your faith, unless you took his."

"No," she said, above the crackle of frying potatoes, "and I'm not marrying into his church. Mormons can take more than one wife, and I'm not rushing home from my honeymoon so my husband can hurry away on another one."

"Why don't you refuse him?"

"Wouldn't do any good. No other boy in the valley dares to come around, knowing how Billy feels about me. Besides, Billy's Mr. Bryce Peyton's first son by his third wife, as I recall, and Billy's trying to persuade his father to send the Mormon children to my school. I'd certainly like to bring those children to the light, at two dollars, apiece, head tax, payable to the teacher."

"Still, the young men in this valley must be lily-livered. Billy ought to have claim jumpers all over the place."

"Billy's a little ornery," she explained. "Most of the boys know I despise violence, and Billy can get violent when he thinks somebody's taking on over me."

She brought his plate and a cup of coffee and set them before him. "Now, when you're through with this chicken, Mr. McCloud, I want your honest opinion if it's the best chicken you ever tasted. If it's not, you needn't say a thing."

"All right, Miss Stewart, but why don't you just call me Ian?"

"I'd be pleased to, Ian, and you may call me Gabriella until Billy gets here. After that, we'd best go back to Mister and Miss because Billy might think we're getting too familiar."

"Is Billy coming here?"

"He will if you have a second cup of coffee. He watches from the saloon across the street."

"I didn't think Mormons drank," Ian said, biting into a chicken leg. It was good chicken, and a sip of the coffee told him he was bound to have a second cup.

"Billy's sort of a backslider, a jackleg as the other Mormons call him." Suddenly her voice grew excited. "Here he comes, already. He must have seen you smile at me, and he's getting worried."

"Well, if I'm not going to have the pleasure of your talk, Gabriella, maybe I could look at your book while I'm eating."

"Why, I'd be pleased, Ian," she said, handing him the book. "I'm always glad to see somebody read an enlightening book. But, remember, call me Miss Stewart, and I hate violence."

"I'll remember, Miss Stewart, and I hate violence, too."

Ian raised his eyes to look at the man who emerged from the swinging doors across the street and disliked instantly what he saw, a tall and handsome young man with a ten-gallon white hat tilted back over his waving and lustrous black hair. There was deviltry in the smile that flashed teeth in the afternoon sun, an animal litheness in the swing of the broad shoulders. The only aspect of the approaching man Ian approved of was the way in which he wore his pearl-handled revolver, strapped low on his thigh with a double thong in the conventional manner of the gunfighter.

The hand had a long way to travel before it reached the pistol's butt. Billy Peyton would be dead before his gun cleared its holster.

Ian glanced down at the book, opened it, and immediately became so engrossed he barely noticed Peyton enter and order a cup of coffee. He failed to notice, entirely, the hostile glance Peyton threw down the counter at him.

Ian was reading. Although unable to decipher the name of the book, *Novum Organum,* he made out most of the words inside. When he discovered that long words were small words put together, he had found a key to a language he recognized as English but which was written in a manner no trailhand ever used and, for that matter, no newspaper. After three pages, he was picking up speed. Almost unconsciously he asked for a second cup of coffee because, after the fifth page, he was breaking out of the chaparral. By the seventh page, he was reading at a full gallop. On page twenty, and his third cup of coffee, he was brought back to his surroundings by the loud voice of Billy Peyton.

"Looks like you got a scholar in here, Gabe, and a real coffee drinker."

Ian looked up the counter toward the man. With intuitive clarity, he realized that his virtuous behavior had availed him nothing; Billy Peyton, grown jealous of a reading ability which would raise a man's standing in the eyes of a schoolteacher, was trying to pick a fight.

Shamefacedly, Ian closed the offending book and shoved it down the counter, as Gabriella tried to wedge polite formality between the two men. "Mr. Peyton, this is Mr. McCloud. He brought in Brother Trotter."

Peyton was not interested in friendly formalities.

"Well, coffee drinker," he said with loud contempt, "you must be a Samaritan."

"No, sir," Ian said politely, "I hail originally from Alabama."

"My, isn't he the witty one." Peyton addressed the girl with mincing tones. "Or maybe your scholar doesn't know that a Samaritan is somebody who does good deeds, like bringing in a dead body before the other buzzards get to it."

Billy Peyton was using grammar, yet he was making out that Ian was a sissy.

"I just did my Christian duty, sir," Ian interposed humbly.

Billy Peyton slapped his exposed thigh and guffawed, still directing his conversation to Miss Stewart. "A Christian as well as a scholar! I bet he's a chicken lover, too."

Billy Peyton was spoiling for a fight. Coming out from under the influence of Francis Bacon, Ian's thoughts swung back into their old channels. If Peyton didn't appreciate virtue and wanted to fight, he was giving Ian a chance to get rid of the horse guard at church tomorrow. But, he cautioned himself, Peyton might be a coward who wore a fancy gun to shore up his courage and he might back away from a showdown. Ian wanted to forestall any backdown. He wanted to kill Peyton fair and square, and it would hurt his currently high standing in the community if he shot a man in the back who was running away.

Ian affected an apologetic look and spoke with a voice that reeked with humility. "I truly do love chicken, Mr. Peyton. I ain't never wrapped my lips around a better breast than Miss Stewart's and her thighs are about as good as any I ever sunk my teeth into."

"What are you talking about, boy?"

"Miss Stewart's chicken, sir."

"Sounded for a minute, there, like you were giving your last will and testament, and maybe you were."

"If I done you any offense, Mr. Peyton, I surely want to apologize. Next to Miss Stewart's chicken, there's nothing I'd like better than a little peace. . . ."

"Watch it, boy!"

In desperation, Ian turned to the girl.

"I do want to thank you for the loan of your book. As Sir Francis Bacon says, 'Some books are to be chewed and digested.' His own is one of them books, and so's your chicken. Now, you got my meal ticket, Ma'am, and you can punch it any way you see fit, but I want to leave this silver dollar with you in appreciation for the most delightful breast, legs, and thighs I ever met with on life's journey."

The silver dollar he laid on the counter was the largest gratuity he had ever left a waitress, but it was a small price to pay for a fast horse. Gabriella plucked it from the counter with delight and excitement, saying, "Why I do appreciate both of them, Mr. McCloud, the speech and the dollar."

Tipping his hat to her deferentially, he walked toward the door, giving Peyton a wide and respectful berth, but politeness availed him little.

"Boy, that *was* your last will and testament."

As Ian eased out of the door, with a shy, scurrying movement, he heard Gabriella exclaim, "Now you leave him be, Billy. Mr. McCloud is a good Methodist."

"A *good* Methodist! Well, that does it."

Ian walked rapidly down the boardwalk toward the hotel. Behind him he heard the door open and close, and he stepped up his pace. Behind him, the clomp of boots on the boardwalk sounded faster.

"Hey, boy!"

Ian did not like the term "boy." Peyton was using it because he was a few inches taller than Ian and not because he was older. But Ian stopped and turned, forcing a smile that wobbled on his face as Billy Peyton halted twenty paces behind him.

"Yes, sir."

"That girl back there. She's my girl."

There was a temporizing, lecturing note in the Mormon's voice. Apparently he was not intending to gun down the respected stranger, only to give a bullying lecture.

"I don't doubt that, Mr. Peyton, but, as I told you, I'm a peace lover. . . ."

"Watch it, boy."

"What I mean, Mr. Peyton, is that I'm no gunfighter like you, partly because I'm peaceful but mostly because I'm so slow. I'm kindly disposed toward everybody, Mr. Peyton. Even Mormons. Maybe mostly Mormons. It's hard enough for a man to make his way in this world when he don't know who his pa is. It's a lot harder for a son like you, whose pa's got fifteen or sixteen wives, because a poor old Mormon boy, like you, don't even know who his ma is."

"You wouldn't be calling me a son of a bitch?"

"No, sir, Mr. Peyton. I couldn't rightly call you one. Only your pa could do that, since he's the only man who knows which bitch is which."

"Draw, Gentile," Billy Peyton snarled.

The men had forced the moment to a crisis. G-7 caught with its tendrils out, diffused along the neutral channels of McCloud, and it knew with the knowledge of its host what devastation might be wrought by a lead slug ripping through brain tissues. Vulnerable, now, it was faced with the instant dissolution of its photons. With it would go all hope for this species, and it was either it or the Mormon.

Reluctantly but instantaneously, G-7 fissioned an ion and slowed the currents of time around Billy Peyton.

With lightning speed the Mormon's hand swooped toward the gun, but the hand had a long way to go to the low-slung pistol, and Ian knew, already, the gunfighter he faced was a rank amateur. Not only had Peyton telegraphed his move by tensing his knees, the fool had yelled at Ian to draw.

This boy, Ian remembered, was the son of Bryce Peyton, the Mormon stake superintendent. Through Billy Peyton, Gabriella was trying to bring the Mormon children to the light. Ian hungered to send a bullet into the groins of Peyton, killing him slowly and letting him know that death was on the way, but his hand slowed at the thought of Gabriella's students.

In its haste, G-7 erred in attempting to superimpose its own unselfish aims onto the purposes of the gunfighter.

With Peyton grabbing iron, this was one hell of a time to be thinking about schoolchildren he cared not a whit about. Far more important to Ian was the opportunity to get rid of the horse guard at the church tomorrow. Besides, with Peyton out of the way, he could drive Gabriella to church, in a springed buggy with a wide, cushioned front seat. He couldn't think of a more pleasant way to spend a Sunday morning than with a girl who liked his speeches and grew ecstatic over silver dollars, schoolteacher or no.

Ian's last musing, drawn out over several microseconds, gave G-7 a clue to more powerful motivational areas in the human psyche. It reacted with whorls of energy around the mating nodules in the man's brain.

McCloud had never heard of Lilith or Helen of Troy. For him, Semiramis had never been, and Deirdre was a lie told by an Irishman. Yet, at this moment with Peyton's hand finally touching the pistol's handle, he felt all the storied charm of earth's immortal beauties, all the nuances of love held by romantic legend, focused in an after-image on his brain of a golden-haired waitress. For approximately three one-hundredths of a second, McCloud was in love with Gabriella Stewart.

He had to take the girl to church tomorrow, but a proper schoolteacher would never permit herself to be escorted by the man who had gunned down her recognized suitor the day before. The problem occurred to Ian simultaneously with its solution. He could make Billy Peyton the laughing stock of Shoshone Flats. He could spare the man but kill his pride.

It was Ian McCloud's solution, not G-7's, but since levity is an attribute of luminosities, the humor in the plan aroused G-7's admiration.

Peyton's revolver had cleared its holster before Ian moved. He flipped out his gun and took careful aim, firing at the index finger protruding from the trigger guard of Peyton's pistol, leading the upward moving target by a quarter-inch. Ian fired. Watching the slug from his .44 move along its trajectory, Ian knew before it had gone six feet that the bullet was on target. No follow-up shot would be necessary.

G-7 did not figure the firing angle for its host. With his nerves, viscera, muscles, and keen eyesight, McCloud had done it all himself, and G-7 was proud of the man.

Ian saw his bullet stride the trigger casing of the Mormon's gun, sever the first two joints of Peyton's trigger finger, and ricochet, tumbling to strike sideways against Peyton's belt buckle. The slow, driving force of the bullet jackknifed Peyton backward along the boardwalk, lifting his boot heels into the air.

Technically Peyton had never fired the bullet which oozed from the muzzle of his revolver and crawled slowly toward a clump of bushes ten paces between the gunfighters; Ian's bullet had fired Peyton's pistol. As Ian watched the .38 slug plummet toward the ground, he made, for him, a strange resolution: He would never tell anyone that his bullet had fired Peyton's pistol. Without doubt, this was Billy Peyton's first and only gunfight, and it was fitting that, along with the stub of his trigger finger, the Mormon be left some tattered remnant of his pride.

As time regained its tempo in the roar of pistols, Ian saw Peyton's gun swirling away into the dust and Billy sitting on the sidewalk holding a bleeding stub of what had once been his trigger finger in front of him, looking at it in disbelief. He saw Gabriella rushing from the restaurant. Across the road, the swinging doors of Bain's saloon swung outward, propelling Mr. Bain and four spavined dance hall girls dressed in ball gowns toward the scene. Sheriff Faust was emerging from his office, rubbing the sleep from his eyes. Down the street, the door of Near-Sighted Charlie's Funeral Parlor opened and a sawed-off man groped his way out. All the images impinged but briefly on Ian's sight as he moved toward his fallen foe, whipping the bandanna from around his neck and twisting it as he advanced.

"Give me your wrist, lead knuckles," he said as he knelt beside the seated man who stared dazedly at the stub of his missing finger which was spurting blood. "I'll tourniquet your arm."

As Ian tightened the handkerchief and the blood flow lessened and stopped, Peyton recovered his senses.

"It'd been better for me if you'd killed me, mister, because I'd like to return your favor, but I won't be able to. I can't pay back a dead man. Gentiles don't gun down saints in this country without retribution, but I will say a little prayer for you while I watch you hang."

"If I ever see you again, you'd better bring this bandanna with you, washed and ironed. You'd better start thinking about taking in washing for a living and forget gunfighting."

"Hey," Near-Sighted Charlie yelled from down the street, "that one for me or for the doc?"

"Get back to Will Trotter, undertaker," Mr. Bain shouted to the sawed-off man who was feeling his way down the boardwalk. "This one's for the doctor."

Gabriella was first to stand above them, her hand clutching her throat, looking down at her suitor's blood in horror as other spectators converged from the general store, smithy shop, post office, hardware store and hotel.

"I saw it all happen, sheriff," Mr. Bain explained as Sheriff Faust walked up. "Peyton drew first, trying to gun down McCloud. His pistol cleared the holster before Mr. McCloud even went for his. Mr. McCloud waited, drew second, and, for Christ's sake, begging Miss Stewart's pardon, took aim and fired before Billy could even pull his trigger. Fastest draw I ever did see, bar none. . . . Stand back, folks. Here comes the doctor."

From his squatting position, holding the tourniquet, Ian saw the crowd form an aisle for the doctor who walked through and looked down.

"He'll be all right, Mr. McCloud," the doctor said. "If you'll let me keep the tourniquet on him, I'll take him down to my place and bandage him up proper."

"Let him keep my bandanna," Ian said, rising. "He got it bloody, so he can wash it."

"That's against my better judgment," the doctor said. "We'll be needing all the bandages we can get when Billy gets word of the shooting back to his pa. . . . You folks had better boil out all the old scraps of linen or cotton you got and have them ready. The Avenging Angels will ride over this. . . . Come on, Billy. I'll treat you like I would a Christian, and you tell your pa I was good to you. You hear?"

As the doctor helped Billy to his feet, a small man with a large head, a black beard, and melancholy brown eyes intoned to the crowd, "Now, death and destruction from the Avenging Angels. Now, the dark saints will ride. Now is the time of woe. Woe to all Gentiles and this Hebrew."

"Oh, hush up, Mr. Bernbaum," Gabriella said to him in vexation. "You always look on the gloomy side of things. All Ian did was to shoot Mr. Peyton's finger off."

She had used, Ian noticed, the familiar address for him and the formal for Billy Peyton. Come Sunday, he might get more from the church meeting than a fast horse.

31

With Peyton blood still on his hands, Ian turned to the voice of Sheriff Faust. "Mr. McCloud, twice today you've done your Christian duty, bringing Will Trotter in and sending Billy Peyton out, but your last good deed might have been one too many. I'm taking the word of Gentile witnesses that the Mormon drew first, so I'm not bringing any charges against you. But I want you to understand that the law's approval don't mean the law's protection. Before the Avenging Angels ride in, my advice to you is to ride out. Mormons don't take kindly to being shot by Gentiles."

"Who are the Avenging Angels, sheriff?" Ian asked.

"It's a Mormon vigilante committee that protects them against us Gentiles, but sometimes the the committee gets a little overzealous about protecting."

"How many vigilantes on that committee?"

"Six. Bryce Peyton and five of his hand-picked saints."

"I ain't worried." Ian shrugged. "I carry a six-shooter."

"If you're bound and determined to stay here for the next stage, not much I can do but warn you. At least you'll see a smiling face when you go out. Superintendent Peyton always smiles when he passes judgment."

"If you feel the need to fortify your courage, son," Mr. Bain said, "drinks are on the house over at my place, if you don't mind drinking in the company of women."

Behind Bain, Ian could see the soft oval of Gabriella's face harden into disapproval.

"I appreciate your offer, Mr. Bain, but I done took the temperance oath."

Gabriella stepped forward. "Ian, don't listen to these calamity howlers and tempters. You're safe, at least till Tuesday. Mr. Peyton won't get to his father's place before midnight, and Mormons don't work on Sunday. Then they won't meet till Monday to take a vote. You come in here with me and wash that blood off your hands."

"Woe, woe unto Shoshone Flats," Mr. Bernbaum intoned.

"It is written, selah. Sodom shall be destroyed and with it all the Sodomites."

Ian let himself be led into the restaurant. As she added more water to the kettle on the stove, Gabriella said, "Ian, using your own bandanna to stance Mr. Peyton's blood was a magnanimous act."

"I hope 'magnanimous' means something nice, Gabriella."

"It does. Magnanimity was the old Roman ideal of behavior. A magnanimous man treats friend or foe with equal compassion. Besides, the way those people were talking, you'd think the Mormons were a bunch of scalawags. They just have the wrong religion, that's all. Of course, Mr. Bryce Peyton hears voices, but, from all I hear, they're reasonable voices. He says they're his angels and he may be right. If the committee decides to hang you, it'll be justice by their lights, and you'll have the satisfaction of knowing you died legally under their law."

She was wrong, he thought, about his magnanimity. Something happened to his head when he took that tumble in the stagecoach. The old Johnny Loco would have killed his best friend over a girl, but Ian McCloud had let a stranger off with nothing more than a nipped finger. When he winged the Mormon, he had not been himself.

"Gabriella," he said, as she fetched a washbasin, "seeing as how your escort won't be able to make it to church tomorrow, I'd be right proud if you'd let me rent a rig and drive you to the meeting."

"Why, Ian, I'd be pleased and honored," she answered, blushing at the spontaneity of her reply. "You come out and have breakfast with mama and me. I'll tell you how to get there, but if you should get lost, anyone in the valley can tell you how to get to Widow Stewart's chicken ranch."

"I'll be there, ma'am washed and shaved."

Something was definitely wrong with his head, he decided. If he had wanted a woman, he should not have waved Bain away when the saloon keeper came piling out of the barroom with four

33

prime, crib-gnawing females already broke and gentled. So why, he wondered, was he planning to wash, shave, and hire a rig for a girl a man would have to court a week before holding her hand?

Ian had lost the answer long ago, in the whine of minié balls and the gut thrusts of bayonets. Violence had borne his gentleness away, but the being within, judging the man with abstract compassion, held him blameless. Ian could relearn gentleness, and the girl with the enigmatic name and delightful lilt to her breasts would be the outlaw's teacher.

With the immaculate honesty of its kind, G-7 admitted to itself that Ian's hormones, reinforcing its ancestral ardor, had led it to choose the girl, but in the matter of Gabriella Stewart, it and its host were functioning as a single entity.

3

FROM his second floor room in Taylor's Hotel, Ian watched the shadows of the Tetons stretch eastward across the valley and fade into night as he listened to "Oh! Susanna," with a dead sound in the middle D, tinkle up from a player piano in Bain's Saloon across the street. Down there, where lamps were being lit, free whiskey awaited him, and he could hear the laughter of women, but he was avoiding company. In fact, he was standing well back from the window—no lamp would be lit in his room tonight—and the back of a chair was propped under the knob of the locked and bolted door to his room.

Yielding to a whim, he stood for a while watching the stars come out and tried to remember the names of the individual stars. He could remember the Big Dipper, the Little Dipper, and the Milky Way, but the only single star he knew by sight was the North Star, which he used to guide on when traveling after dark. He turned away from the window in disgust, not at his faulty memory but at himself for idling away his time trying to remember things that didn't really matter.

He spread a pallet on the floor at the foot of the bed, facing the door. If any of Billy Peyton's friends who were familiar with the layout of the room fired through the door at a point where the sleeper should be, they would have had two chances to become bushwhackers, their first and their last.

From where he lay, finally, spread-eagled on the pallet, his pistol near his hand, he could see the stars through the window. In the reveries of beginning sleep, the Milky Way reminded him of the swash of freckles beneath the eyes of Gabriella, and the image arrested his glide into somnolence. Impatiently he brushed the vision from his mind, vaguely disturbed by the turns his thoughts were taking. Here he lay, moping over stars and a girl, when he should have been thinking about a fast horse, a bank, and about getting out of Shoshone Flats before a passel of angry Mormons came swarming out of the lower valley.

Ian slept.

G-7 never slept. Now it took a long-delayed opportunity to evaluate the data which had been pouring into its host all day to reflect on its growing knowledge of man. There was very much planning to be done.

The scout was aware of strange, bug-eyed monsters slithering in the depth of space. It remembered the snails on the eighteenth planet of Vega spewing venom before them to grease their paths with carrion. G-7 had individually converted the hookfangs of Vulpecula 8 who used torture as a religious ritual, but it had met no species comparable to the humans of sun 3 who had learned to walk upright in order to use their forelegs for maiming and destroying their own and other species.

Yet the scout was not completely overcome with revulsion. Objectivity was a gift of its ethereality, and experience had taught it versatility. It had to admit that this organism was superbly conditioned to its environment, and G-7 was accustomed to working with whatever material was at hand. Nothing in its code condoned the willful destruction or impairment of energy systems, but, on the other hand, it knew that sometimes good could be the final goal of ill.

This superb engine of destruction, Ian McCloud, could never be driven to light, never directly led—G-7 had fissioned an ion to prevent the murder of Billy Peyton—only nudged toward goodness at an oblique angle. G-7 faced the problem head-on; man was simply not a light-seeking animal and its chosen specimen was even less so. As it nudged Ian toward righteousness, it would have to keep the man's eyes averted. Metaphysically speaking, the light from a single candle might prove a blinding glare to Ian McCloud.

To train the man to lead the human race, it would first be necessary to persuade McCloud to join the human race while making full use of his genius for violence which elevated him above a species which evinced merely a general talent for mayhem.

By now, G-7 had spotted areas in the social order of human beings where a man of McCloud's inclinations might function, if not with virtue at least with legality, particularly if that man, as in the case of Bryce Peyton, had an angel to blame for his errors. G-7 was intrigued by the Mormon concept of angels, and it sensed that McCloud, with his forcibleness, might be the ideal instrument for bringing the opposing religious factions in the valley together and for lighting a flame in this small town which might someday illuminate the entire planet.

Gabriella might assist G-7 in placing the outlaw onto a path toward legality, particularly if she were favorably impressed by tomorrow's spooning, and G-7 was already determined to add its bit to the preservice festivities—purely for self-educational purposes. G-7 had deduced a working knowledge of the species reproductive methods from McCloud's fantasies in the restaurant, but it needed practical experience and its own curiosity had been aroused by the girl. When she walked, the middle part of her swayed with the lightness of a wavering luminosity, and there was an evanescence in the perky uplift of her breasts. . . .

G-7's host stirred and twitched, and the being quickly withdrew a strumming tendril from a sensitive area of the man's thalamus.

With Ian quieted, G-7 considered a paradox.

On a planet of such limitless energy, romance and fertilization should have been combined into a single spontaneity of blithe and unpremeditated art. The impulse toward union was so strong in McCloud that he would have been the crown prince of pollinators on a sexually liberated planet such as Vulvula, but McCloud had been strangely timid around the female. G-7 had encouraged the man to be polite to the woman because politeness toward women was a part of the law-abiding syndrome, but it had not expected such powerful constraint, particularly around a female who literally burned to be ravished by him.

The woman's attitudes confused G-7 even more. Her flesh was willing, but her spirit was weak. She had leaped at the opportunity to go to church with a wayfaring stranger, not out of concern for the wayfarer's spiritual welfare, as she so piously told herself, but from a covert yearning for the stranger's body. Why covert, it wondered. Why deny love, the first law of the universe? It was written that the chalice of love should never be lidded by piety, for that, in the Code, was hypocrisy.

G-7 would explore the enigma of womankind more fully tomorrow. Tonight it would explore the mind of its host and alleviate the man's obsession with revenge. Swinging webs over dendrites, nets between lacunae, G-7 flagellated a cluster of neurons at the base of Ian's thalamus and waited to seine for his dreams.

Along well-worn neutral paths the dreams came. In clarity and with realism, Ian hunkered again in the shadows of a moonlit ravine to hear a tall, thin man in a gray uniform on a gray horse mouth again the insult which sent the sleeper into paroxysms of dream rage so violent the words were unintelligible to G-7.

The sleeper stirred and G-7 withdrew its tracers. The clue to the man's obsession was locked securely in his subconscious. To soothe the sleeper's unease, G-7 stroked the area of pleasant dreams and conjured up a vision of Gabriella.

Immediately, Ian was back in his old ravine, this time with

the seraphic form of Gabriella standing approvingly behind him as he pumped bullet after bullet from a magic pistol into the skeletal form of Colonel Blicket, which writhed and grimaced but did not fall. Delighted by his magic weapon, Ian fired ten, twelve, eighteen. . . .

He bolted awake, grabbing his pistol, as a volley of revolver shots sounded from the street. Even as his grip settled on the pistol's handle, Ian relaxed. Some of the boys were bidding Sheriff Faust a good night as they galloped past his office riding home from the saloon, firing their pistols in defiance of the posted order not to fire weapons inside the town limits.

Ian rolled over and went back to sleep, thinking that the sheriff had erred in posting an ordinance with the word "please" in it. Western folks sometimes took politeness as a sign of weakness, particularly young buckaroos like Billy Peyton.

Morning brought a misting rain. Driving south in a rented buggy toward the widow's ranch, Ian enjoyed the snugness and comfort of the enclosed vehicle and found himself looking forward to seeing Gabriella in her Sunday finery. If it weren't for the long hours and low pay, he thought, it might be pleasant to be a law-abiding citizen.

Widow Stewart's ranch house was a frame building with a vine-shaded front porch standing near the bluff of a cottonwood-bordered ravine. Besides the ordinary appurtenances of a ranch house—stable, corral, pump house, privy, washpot, and clothesline—a row of hen houses sat twenty yards behind the house in a chicken yard. When Ian knocked, the Widow Stewart answered the door.

Aproned and smiling, she beckoned him in, saying, "Welcome, Ian McCloud. Daughter's still primping. She'll be in the parlor directly, and I'd like to tell you, now, you've made an impression on that girl, and her mother's not so old she can't see why."

Widow Stewart must have had her daughter while still very young, and Ian wasn't so old he couldn't see why. Her high-piled hair was dark and wavy, with pink ears protruding below. Her skin was fairer than Gabriella's with no freckles marring its whiteness. Though no taller than Gabriella, she was wider, except around the waist, and much thicker in places. Her bubbling speech matched her figure. As she took Ian's hat to hang on the coat tree, she bubbled fore and aft.

Whirling to face him again, in several disparate but enchantingly liquid movements, she said, "Have a seat and make yourself comfortable. Do you like your eggs scrambled or fried? One thing we have here is fresh eggs. Folks say the only way to get fresher eggs than the Widow Stewart's is to lay them yourself."

"Scrambled will be fine, ma'am."

"I scramble them with a little cream to give them lightness, and I can drop in some chopped green onions to give them a he-man flavor."

"Just the cream, ma'am. I don't want any man flavor spoiling a hen's eggs."

She threw him a sidelong, coquettish smile, and said, "You sound appreciative, Ian. They say the way to a man's heart is through his stomach, and maybe that's true for both sexes, one way or the other."

Turning with a wide swing to her well-rounded bottom, she bubbled into the kitchen.

G-7 was overwhelmed by the widow's voluptuousness, vivacity, and contrasting colors, but there was a quality to the woman, observed and dismissed by Ian with maddening superficiality, that almost sent G-7 into a flux; Mrs. Stewart had about her an aura of waiting and wanting, like the plowed loam of springtime, a quality which though apart from her beauty, reinforced it like the pauses in music.

Nothing cowardly or hypocritical impeded the flow of the widow's love system. Through the fibers of its host, G-7 had felt the woman's pull, and, more than its host, it appreciated the electromagnetic vortices swirling around breast gravities whose amplitudes left Ian unstirred. Perhaps McCloud, because of his professional reliance on fast horses, was more appreciative of lean flanks, G-7 mused, whereas itself, a star rover, was more aesthetically aware of world lines. Whatever the cause, it was apparent to G-7 that on this planet it was a breast angel while its host was a thigh man.

"Good morning, Ian."

Ian was brought to his feet by the appearance of Gabriella. Framed in the doorway, she wore a pink gown which flowed to her ankles from a sash of white ribbon around her waist and a hat, wide-brimmed and yellow. Almost gasping at the vision, Ian managed to stammer, "Good morning, Miss Stewart."

Not unaware of his reaction, she blushed slightly.

"I tried on a new hat for you. It's glazed straw, and I thought it might be best for rainy weather. Do you like it?"

"Ma'am I ain't seen no hat half so pretty in all my life. If one drop of rain touches that hat, I'll gun the raindrop down."

She smiled at his witticism, lifting the hat to fluff her curls, and said, "Now, wouldn't you just know it would rain."

"It's just misting a little, ma'am. Not enough to get your shoe tops wet if your ankles stick out from under the buggy top."

Somewhat shyly they both stood and talked for several minutes about the weather, of its danger to the health of her mother's chickens and the possibility that the dry gulch behind the house might overflow and flood the hen houses. Between them they tugged and stretched the subject of the rain in a pleasant, conversational taffy pull until the widow reentered the parlor.

"My, what a handsome matched pair you two make," she said, breaking the spell. "But breakfast is ready."

G-7 caught dissonances in the older woman's voice as she complimented the two, a subtle conflict of interests which Ian must have detected.

"Mrs. Stewart, I just got to stand here, flatfooted, and tell you, you got a daughter no woman in Wyoming can compare with but her mother."

"Oh, bother!" Mrs. Stewart stammered. "You flatter me,

but I can't say I don't like it. Now, come and get it. I've fixed a man-sized breakfast for a real man: scrambled eggs, flapjacks, smoked bacon, sausage, souse meat, red-eye gravy, grits, hot buttered biscuits with jelly and jam, and all the coffee you can drink. It ought to hold us till after we get back from church. Then I'm going to fix you the best fried chicken dinner you ever tasted."

He had forgotten that respectable girls were chaperoned, but, strangely, her reminder did not disturb him. He stood back to let the contrast in feminine pulchritude precede him into the kitchen-dining room, comparing the sway of Miss Stewart to the bounce of Mrs. Stewart.

Only one flaw marred the grandeur of the colossal breakfast. In the formal atmosphere of a courtship, Ian found the terms of address, "Miss Stewart" and "Mrs. Stewart," somewhat tongue twisting.

Mrs. Stewart righted the matter. "Heck, Ian. Just call her Gabe and me Liza. I feel like I've known you for twenty years, or maybe I feel like I'd have felt meeting you twenty years ago."

"But, mother," Gabriella protested, "it wouldn't be proper for Brother Winchester's congregation to hear me called Gabe. I can't let those people get too familiar, since I have to birch their children, sometimes twice a day."

In the hour of breakfast, Ian found that Brother Winchester, the Methodist preacher, was also the mayor of Shoshone Flats during the weekdays and that people had been looking forward all week to his sermon, "What Heaven Is Like," because Brother Winchester was so good at giving his congregation hell. Ian also learned that Brother Will Trotter's body was being kept on ice and his funeral delayed until Wednesday because of a church picnic on Tuesday which all the non-Mormons in the valley would attend.

Liza had heard of Ian's gunfight with Billy Peyton and offered him the protection of her chicken ranch. "I got a long bore shotgun, and if the Mormons come, I'd be a lot more help than Sheriff Faust. If you want to put up here with us and go to the picnic Tuesday, I guarantee you'll be safe with me."

Although Ian planned to leave Monday, he reflected on Liza's invitation that he stay here with "us" and be protected by "me." Maybe Liza figured if he stayed here over Monday, while Gabriella was in town running the restaurant, she might beat her daughter's time with Ian. Strangely, the idea intrigued him, though not enough to divert him from his purposes.

"Thank you, Liza, but I ain't scared of Mormons. Anyhow, I ain't educated enough to hide out with a schoolteacher and her mama."

"Ignorance, that's for me," the widow said. "I never read a book in my life, excepting one Gabe made me read about a woman with a house full of girls, a book writ by somebody named Louisa Allcock. . . ."

"Alcott, mother."

". . . who didn't know mountain oysters about raising girls. . . . Gabe's father was a great reader, and Gabe inherited the family curse. Reading's what got her pa killed."

"Mother! You know daddy died in a fall from a horse."

Horrified reproach in the daughter's voice stopped the pell-mell speech of her mother abruptly, and Ian filled the embarrassed silence with a comment. "I ain't never read much, myself, excepting McGuffey's books."

He hoped the remark would put an end to book talk because literary discussions embarrassed him, but Gabriella would not let his modesty go unchallenged.

"You were doing all right with Bacon's essays."

"Yes'm but I thought he was a cookbook."

The widow had been weighing a course of action which she took. "Gabe don't want me to talk about her pa, but I feel I got to warn you anyhow—reading can kill you."

Feeling he was forced to take sides, Ian tried to balance himself between the two women. "Yes'm, I reckon, though I ain't heard of anybody getting gunned down by a book."

"You almost saw it done to Billy Peyton," Liza corrected

him. "He drawed on you because he wanted to be like them dead-eye Dicks in the dime novels he reads to impress Gabe. . . . Her curse is catching, Ian. Reading most nigh got her beau killed. John Milton killed her pa."

"Mother!" Gabe's exclamation was an order the widow obeyed.

It was plain to him that there was a skeleton in this family's closet, but he accepted the knowledge with equanimity. There was a skeleton in the McCloud family's closet, and he was it. At the moment he was more curious about this John Milton, a gunfighter he had never heard of, and he was even more intrigued by the thought processes of the widow. She might well be right about Billy Peyton, whom Ian had already suspected of being jealous of his own reading ability. For an ignorant, uneducated woman, the widow had a good head on her shoulders.

"Leastways," Liza continued, "the Alcott woman didn't know doodly squat about the tribulations of a widow raising an orphaned daughter."

Ian listened sympathetically as Liza outlined the problems of bringing up a daughter without a man around to help, but inwardly he didn't feel too sympathetic. Her husband had been dead for less than a year, had died after Gabriella had started to teach school, and Liza seemed to be doing well with a four-room house, a chicken ranch, and the family restaurant.

Still, to commiserate, he suggested that she might sell boxed chicken lunches to the stage passengers to eat on the road. "Give Mr. Birnie two cents' commission on each twenty-five cent box, and he'll sell the boxes for you, maybe put them on the cost of a stage ticket."

"One cent would do it, Ian. By golly, that just shows you what the guidance of a man can do for a poor widow woman. I'll corner the old skinflint in church this morning. If you decide to settle in Shoshone Flats, I'll cut you in for a nickel a box just for the idea."

He thanked her for her generosity and told her if it wasn't that he had to get back to El Paso and his cattle-buying office, he would take her up on the offer.

Liza, with her appreciation for men and her quick head for making money, would make some cowpoke a good mother-in-law, Ian thought. As a matter of fact, Liza, with her common sense and enthusiasm, and Gabriella, with her book learning and modesty, would make some Mormon a well-balanced pair of wives.

No. It would never do for the Gentile mother and daughter to wed the same Mormon. Gabe was too sensitive to be married to her stepfather. Any son of hers by the man would be her stepbrother, which would make Gabriella, as the stepsister of her own son, her own stepmother, and Gabe was too young to have an eighteen-year-old stepdaughter. Ian realized the idea was whimsical, but the speed at which he made the interfamilial connections amazed him. The tumble in the stagecoach had reshuffled his brain and stacked the deck.

He relished the breakfast, down to the last grit and last dab of red-eye gravy. Afterward, seated between the two women on the drive to church, he found them equally enjoyable. Lithe Gabriella sat modestly apart, telling of the need for a better school house for Shoshone Flats, while Liza, with her greater spread, talked man-and-woman talk with thigh pressure. Yes, he thought, they were a well-matched span of females.

It was still drizzling when they reached the church, and Ian was disappointed to see only one riding horse hitched to the church rack. Most of the families had come in covered buggies pulled by driving horses, and the one saddle horse present seemed to have been chosen to spare some nobler beast the rigors of bad weather.

Because of the rain, arriving members of the congregation were being greeted in the vestibule by Brother Winchester, the preacher-mayor, rifle straight and ramrod thin, whose gun-metal eyes glinted with pleasure when he met Ian.

"Welcome, Brother McCloud. I've heard about your good deeds already, and I hope this visit to our town won't be your last. If the Lord sees fit to give you the courage to stay over till

Tuesday, we'd be grateful to have you at our church picnic. It's being held down close to the Mormon's stake boundary. If any of the saints ride over to join us in Christian fellowship, some of the brothers will be bringing their rifles to welcome them, but we could use your pistol. Sister Liza's furnishing the chicken hampers for our picnic."

Sister Liza reached over and gave Ian a maternal hug.

"I'm giving him a sample for dinner. If that won't persuade him to stay over for our picnic, he's beyond salvation."

"With your permission, Brother McCloud," the preacher said, "I'd like to introduce you to the congregation before the sermon and ask you to say a few words."

"He'd better, Reverend," Gabriella enjoined, vying with her mother to give Ian a conversational hug, "because I want to show him off."

"Well, preacher," Ian said, "I don't see how I can refuse, but I'm a mite shy around crowds and might not say much."

"Just tell us a little something about yourself, son, and say a few complimentary words about our town."

Entering the pew, Liza politely motioned him ahead of her so she wouldn't come between him and Gabriella, and she whispered, "Brother Winchester's running for mayor again next June. That's why he'd like for you to say something nice about the town."

"You say what you think, Ian," Gabriella said. "After all, you have to live with your conscience. You don't have to lie, even for a preacher."

"I'll tell the truth," Ian said.

So he came to be seated between two of the loveliest Gentiles in the Shoshone Flats Methodist Church, and, in his opinion, the three of them made a good singing trio as he held the hymnal for the opening hymn. Mother and daughter had to lean toward him to read the words as they sang, and he found Gabriella's perfume helped him on the high notes, whereas he favored Liza's when reaching for the low notes.

After the plate was passed and Ian was divested of another of

Brother Trotter's silver dollars, Brother Winchester introduced Ian with the words, "It's not yet time to eulogize our late Brother William Trotter. I'll be doing that, Wednesday, at two P.M., but I would like to introduce and compliment the man who brought Brother Trotter in—Mr. Ian McCloud."

Ian arose to polite applause. Looking out over the congregation, he spoke in a strong but modest voice. "I'm happy to be here, folks. I didn't come under the best conditions, but I've been well treated by the merchants of Shoshone Flats, with one exception. One of the best things about your town is the chicken served in Miss Stewart's Restaurant, furnished by the Widow Stewart. One of the worse things is the aim of your Mormon gunfighters. Howsomever, I think Dead Man's Curve could use a little straightening."

"You tell 'em, Ian McCloud!" A female voice screamed from the rear, and Ian knew it came from beneath a sunbonnet.

"Amen, or second the motion," a masculine voice responded.

"I been traveling that road for twenty years," the banshee wail continued, "and the only thing that's gonna straighten it out is a new mayor for Shoshone Flats."

"Sister Betsy, control yourself," the preacher said. "There's an administrative problem here, which the average citizen can't be expected to understand; namely, who's going to pay the labor?"

"Preacher," Ian said helpfully, "why not use the jail prisoners in a road gang."

"There ain't no prisoners, Brother McCloud. Our good sheriff, Brother Faust, is as strong a believer in brotherly love, even when it's against the town's policy. But I thank you and welcome you to Shoshone Flats. My sermon for today is 'Heaven as It Really Is.' "

Ian sat down as the preacher jumped quickly into his sermon. After fifteen minutes, Ian figured it might be time to excuse himself and go steal the horse, but a flurry of rain on the roof made him reconsider. Hiding out in weather like this, all night, waiting for the bank to open, could give a man lung congestion, and the lone saddle horse at the hitching rack didn't look like much of a mudder. If he waited for the evening services, the weather might clear, and clearing weather would also give him a better selection of horses.

Also, Ian was beginning to pay attention to the sermon, and, for reasons he could not understand, was even growing interested.

Brother Winchester was describing the sights and sounds of heaven, beginning with the first sweet notes of Gabriel's trumpet.

"Ah, sweet music to the ears of the saved, brothers and sisters, but a dirge unto the damned."

He got past the golden gate in fine style, describing it with a jeweler's attention to the details, but when he came to describing the throne of God, either his vision failed him or his voice faltered. "Pure radiance, brothers and sisters, shimmering, ineffable, surrounded by luminous flights of angels enwrapped in righteous robes of peace."

Inside Ian, G-7 listened tensely. This earthman was giving a literal description of a launching pad with waiting pilots on a stand-by detail.

And Winchester's human audience was straining to catch every dip and quaver of his voice when the preacher made a political error. "I tell you, brothers and sisters, I half-envy the soul of our late Brother Trotter, which, at this very minute, is walking up to that throne of radiance and all enveloping peace. Brother Trotter is done forever with life's toil. For him, no more the ordeal of facing winter's rages atop a coach seat, no more the fear of stage robbers, no more the toiling on the long upgrades, the breaking on the downgrades . . ."

"And no more Dead Man's Curve," Betsy Troop shrilled from the rear. "Ian McCloud for mayor."

"No more the taunts of men, the bile of females, nor the scorn that civic merit from the nonvoter takes," Winchester continued. His righteous wrath closed the breech, and a few of the women began to sob audibly as he swung back to the safer fields of heaven.

Whatever his faults as a mayor, Ian decided, Winchester was a spellbinding preacher, and he proved it at the close of the sermon. Repentance of sin was the key to paradise, he said, and he invited his audience forward to the alter to kneel and pray for forgiveness of their sins. He built his plea up to a final adjuration, "Now the time has come, brothers and sisters, to come forward and confess to Jesus and be saved. Come to Jesus, now, you sinners."

On the word "now" the organist began the old hymn, "Come to Jesus Now," but a quick-step march would have been more appropriate for the congregation. Almost as a body, it rose and went forward, with Liza Stewart leading the procession, and it was good that Liza should lead, Ian thought, because anyone in front of her would have been trampled in her rush to get to the altar. Gabriella sat pat.

"Are you going forward?" Ian asked the girl.

"Schoolteachers don't sin," she said. "But you go ahead, if you're a mind to."

"I'm a little shy about such things," he admitted, "but Liza don't seem backwards. She was pounding leather to get up there, and she don't seem sinful to me."

"A woman can think sinful thoughts," Gabriella said, "and if my mother's asking forgiveness for what I think she's been thinking, well, I never!"

Ian could almost hear Gabriella's jaws snap shut with indignation, and he hastened to comfort her. "Gabriella, she can't even think sinful thoughts out there on the ranch with nothing but them chickens."

"You don't know mama!"

Brother Winchester was moving among his kneeling flock, bending to whisper words of inspiration and faith to each sinner. Ian noticed that his ministrations over Liza were somewhat prolonged, and, in the middle of the church, Ian had a sinful thought regarding the preacher's motives, but Winchester's show of forgiveness seemed to soften Gabriella.

"You can help Sister Liza, Brother Ian," she said, "by not looking at her as if you were studying her and by not saying complimentary things to her. Help her be strong, Brother Ian, for mama is weak."

"Yes'm," Ian promised, slightly addled.

"Now, if you wish to go up and join the others, Brother Ian, I'll understand, but don't kneel next to mama."

It wasn't shyness that restrained Ian but his schedule. If he went forward and confessed his sins, he might be here until Tuesday and he was leaving Monday morning.

"No, Gabriella, I come with you and I'm staying with you."

Suddenly she reached over and patted the back of his hand, saying, "You *are* strong, Ian."

Even as he thrilled to her touch, he thrilled more to the knowledge that there was something of her mother in Gabriella Stewart.

After the sermon, there was a brief fellowship period over coffee in the kitchen at the rear of the church. As the ladies gathered in one room to plan picnic hampers and as Liza corraled Mr. Birnie in an isolated corner, the men gathered around Brother Winchester to thank him for his soul-saving effort and for setting their feet on the path of salvation.

Ian took advantage of the temporary freedom from females to engage the preacher in a theological discussion.

"For some reason, sir, I feel a powerful interest in this Angel Gabriel. Some of the best people I know are named for him. Where does he hail from?"

"From heaven, son, out beyond the stars. He's a powerful man in heaven, an archangel. Some folks think he might have had something to do with Jesus since he was seen calling on Mary just before Christ was born."

"Where'd he get the name Gabriel?"

"Some Hebrew called him by the name and it stuck."

"Does the name mean anything in Hebrew?"

"Can't say since I'm not a Hebrew. You might ask Abe Bernbaum. He's a Hebrew."

"Is he the little fellow with the big head and the deep voice?"

"Yes, sir," the preacher smiled. "He's Shoshone Flats' naysayer and woe-bearer, but he's God's own tailor, the town's official tailor, in fact."

Suddenly the preacher paused and dropped his head in a meditation so deep Ian felt he might be going to sleep on his feet, but he quickly aroused himself.

"Brother McCloud, when I was walking among them sinners, the Holy Ghost asked me to give you a proposal in my capacity as town mayor. We've got Brother Faust as sheriff, but he's a little too old and too Christian for a lawman. If you'd consent to abide with us for a while and act as his deputy, I know a young man with your spunk and grit could help bring law and order to Shoshone Flats and get us enough prisoners to straighten out that curve and maybe fill in a few chuckholes in the road. Of course, we ain't the richest town in the world. We couldn't afford to pay you much, but there are other benefits. As the law, you'd have full protection of the law when the Avenging Angels ride against you, you'd get a brand-new suit of clothes at the town's expense, a free burial preached by me if you should come to an untimely end, and you'd get the loan of a saddle and a fast horse."

Ian became alert at the mention of a fast horse, but immediately he spotted a loophole in the mayor's argument. "The nag you issued to Sheriff Faust looks pretty spavined to me."

"We issue the horse to fit the man," Winchester explained. "Brother Hendricks, the best Gentile horse breeder in the valley, supplies the town with its horses, and he has a genius for matching the horse to the man."

Ian's thinking was assisted by a gust of rain on the roof. With a fast horse under him and the town emptied of people on Tuesday, he'd have the perfect arrangement for holding up the bank. Meanwhile, he'd have the use of the hotel room tonight and Monday night, so he wouldn't have to get wet.

"How much does the job pay?" He feigned an interest.

"Eight dollars a week, but you can bed down in the jailhouse, and the town pays for your meals, either at the restaurant or the saloon, depending on whether you like chicken or steak. We'd like to pay more, but the town's treasury is low."

Suddenly the solution of a problem he did not intend to solve lay clear in Ian's mind. He said, "Mr. Mayor, I could build you a road, pay myself fifteen dollars a week, and add to the town's treasury without costing the town a penny, if you'd let me appoint the justice of peace."

"Well, son"—the mayor rubbed his jaw—"that might cause legal problems. I'm supposed to appoint the justice of peace—we've had no use for one with Sheriff Faust—and the city charter won't let me pay over eight dollars a week to a deputy because the high sheriff only makes eight dollars and two bits."

"I don't know nothing about legal problems," Ian said, "but I can solve them two. You appoint the justice of peace I ask you to appoint and, instead of raising my salary, give me a percentage of all the fines the justice of peace collects."

"Brother McCloud, you've just earned yourself a position of responsibility in the thriving community of Shoshone Flats. . . .

"Brother Hendricks," he called over Ian's shoulder, "I want you to come over and meet our new deputy sheriff, Brother Ian McCloud. What kind of horse can you offer him?"

Brother Hendricks, the horse breeder, advanced with a limp. Ian saw that the man had once been tall and rawboned, but he was bent now from a curvature of the spine, and his right shoulder was a huge lump. Cocking his head, he looked up to Ian from beneath brows corrugated with scar tissue. He was studying the man.

"I'd match him with Midnight," he said finally. "Midnight's as fast as greased lightning, mister. If he can't throw you, he pinwheels and crushes you. If he can throw you, he'll stomp you to death. He's a killer horse, but, by the holy jumping Jehoshaphat, the horse has got spirit!"

"Sounds like my kind of horse," Ian said.

On the ride home, under a misting sky, Gabriella was excited over Ian's appointment. Strangely, Liza, who was experiencing her own elation over a successful move to furnish lunch boxes to the Territorial Stage Lines—one cent going to Birnie and five to Ian—did not share her daughter's enthusiasm.

"All Brother Winchester's doing is getting rid of Ian so he won't run for mayor. Once you've built the road, Ian, he'll take credit and get himself reelected."

With strange detachment, Ian saw the truth in what she said, but he saw deeper to another truth: a mayor indebted to a law officer might become the tool of his own lieutenant. Yet it was a matter that wouldn't concern him after Tuesday.

"I reckon you're right, Liza, but I ain't intending to run for mayor, and if I'm going to load up that jail with lawbreakers, them criminals have got to be fed. As long as the Territorial Stage Lines agreed on a lunch box price, the town of Shoshone Flats will figure it's getting a bargain, and I calculate I'll be needing over a hundred a week. Of course, I ain't much good at sums."

"Nonsense, Ian McCloud," Liza ejaculated, "you're a genius as well as a he-man."

"Oh, mother. Don't be so obvious."

"One thing you have to say about me, daughter, is that I'm grateful. After we've had the chicken dinner I promised you, Ian, I'm inviting you to stay for supper. I'll fix you some of the best chicken dumplings you ever et."

Already Ian was beginning to feel over-chickened, especially now that he knew more solid meat was available at the saloon.

"No'm. I appreciate it, but I got to write some letters to El Paso, and I got to take this rig back to the livery stable, so I'll have to turn down your kind invitation to supper."

All these people were going to a lot of trouble, he thought, just to help him steal a fast horse and rob their bank, but they were getting something back. False hope wasn't much, but it was better than no hope at all.

Despite its triumph at the church meeting, G-7 was disappointed.

Aware that the patterns of man's fate were seldom accidental, it was pleased to have elicited the correct responses from Ian at the services, and it knew that one step at a time was the most it could hope to accomplish in leading the man to legality, but fascinating educational bypaths were opening to it, right here on the buggy's seat, and its host was ignoring them.

Both females were competing for Ian's amorous attention. Yet G-7 knew that the romance it had hoped to research was going to be postponed, partly because of the inhibitions aroused in Ian by the presence of the girl's mother, a presence which actually more than doubled the area of experimentation, partly because of the rain, but mostly because Ian was preoccupied with a five-cent rebate on a twenty-five cent box lunch for nonexistent prisoners. Somehow the prospect of the former Johnny Loco tapping the public till appealed to McCloud's ironic humor.

Love of money was the root of this man's evil. Seated between two women, both eager and the older one willing, he dreamed of theoretical profits and of real cash waiting in a bank to be robbed. Even after his psychic lust was appeased and his thoughts turned from profits, they did not turn to the women beside him.

He thought of a stallion called Midnight. Any horse that liked to kill men was bound to be a spirited steed. Moreover, with his freshly activated neural cells G-7 had quickened for high moral purposes, McCloud had hit on a plan to break the stallion of its pinwheeling habits forever.

4

IAN canceled his planned steak supper at Bain's saloon. Shyness, politeness, and susceptibility to Liza's persuasiveness had led him to eat three extra helpings of fried chicken, and, by the time the overburdened mare pulled him the muddy way into town, the torpor of digestion left him indifferent to food. From the livery stable he went directly to the hotel. Spreading his pallet beneath the gray light from the window, he took the Gideon's Bible from the dresser and sprawled beneath the window to leaf through the pages.

Not once did he speculate about his unusual desire to read the Bible, because the unnatural act fitted well into his extraordinary day. Consciously, he knew only that he wanted to read something, anything. This morning he had been embarrassed to admit in the presence of a schoolteacher that he had read so little, and what reading he had done never led him to the opinion that it was dangerous, as Liza averred.

Still, Liza had a point. Billy Peyton's dime novels and his jealousy toward Bacon had cost the Mormon a finger. Ian could not understand why John Milton would gun down the widow's husband for reading a book—the widow, yes; John Milton, no—but he could understand that there might be indirect perils to the pastime. Reading in the half light of a cloudy afternoon might weaken a gunfighter's eyes and eventually get him killed.

Above and beyond Ian's educational embarrassment, which was accompanied by a sense of futility—he realized that at this late date any attempt to shore up his ignorance would be the equivalent of a limber finger in a very porous dike—he was impelled to the Bible by a peculiar interest which, somehow, seemed natural. Ordinarily, his interest in celestial beings was equal to, but did not exceed, his interest in hagiology. Winchester's description of angels as beings of light had stirred his curiosity, and, in effect, he was unconsciously checking Winchester's sources for the preacher's report on the halo effect.

Now that he was getting the hang of reading, he skimmed through the "begats" of the Old Testament, finding few references to heaven and fewer to angels. In Genesis, however, he paused for a long moment to consider a passage:

> And it came to pass . . . that the sons of God saw the daughters of men and found them fair; and they took them wives of all which they chose.

The man's eyes had found a clue to a mystery the man was not even aware of, and Ian thought he paused over the passage to consider the mechanical problems involved in such an arrangement. From his very limited knowledge of angels, he did not think they were equipped for marriage, but he was not one to argue against the Bible.

Also, he did not know that he regarded the paragraph as a reliquary for an ancient truth.

With varying degrees of interest he read on through twenty-one books of the Bible until, as the still-clouded sun moved toward setting and the day waned outside the window, he came to Solomon's Song. He muttered aloud, "No wonder this hombre had a thousand wives."

Here was raw material aplenty for courting a schoolteacher,

though some of it was a little too raw; he could never tell Gabriella his bowels were moved for her. Sometimes the language was a little too less or too much. Gabriella's breasts were not like those of a young roe; she could give a few inches to any deer he had seen. And her face was not as terrible as an army with banners, not to a man who had lain behind the breastworks at Marye's Heights and watched the blue-bellied Yankees climb the hill. Still, allowing for the lapses, Solomon was a master of sweet talk.

Reluctantly Ian closed the book and laid it aside. Further reading would strain his eyes, and a lighted lamp in the room might reveal him to some Mormon sharp-shooter outside with a rifle. Laying his pistol atop the Bible, he spread-eagled on the pallet, hearing the beginning tinkle of Bain's piano with the "plonk" on the middle D and thinking of the breasts of women. Whoever Solomon sang to must have been more like Gabe than Liza, else Solomon wouldn't have spent so many compliments on thighs and navels. The widow's bosom would have hogged the works, for verily, her breasts were like melons, Stone Mountain watermelons.

Visions of watermelons flowed so naturally into Ian's mind he found the thought no more unusual than his session with the Bible, or the after-feeling that he had been searching the Scriptures for something more definite than spiritual guidance or salvation. He yawned and stretched, thinking: Next to killing Colonel Blicket, there's nothing I'd like better than a piece of watermelon.

At six in the morning Ian awakened, resolved to carry out Sunday's plan; get deputized this Monday; bust a bronc, rob the bank on Tuesday; then ride out of the deserted town on the fastest horse in Wyoming. He drank half a glass of water for breakfast and walked over to the sheriff's office. Following the sound of snores, he found Sheriff Faust asleep in a jail cell at the rear of the building.

Ian reached down and shook the man awake. Faust opened his eyes, raised himself on one elbow, and asked, "Huh?"

"Winchester sent me over to get deputized. You're looking at your new deputy."

Faust listened, lay back, and spoke with his eyes closed, "Go take an inventory of the armory, then look over the wanted posters on my desk. File them according to real name, not alias, and try to memorize the descriptions. Soon as I wake up, I'll swear you in."

Faust resumed snoring.

Ian walked forward between twin rows of cells, four cells on each side with one bunk to the cell, and his mind continued to attack the problem he was not yet committed to solving. If he were to build the road for Shoshone Flats, a jail housing eight men would not be big enough for the twelve or fourteen men he would need on the work gang, unless some of the prisoners slept on the floor.

Ian looked into the armory, an upright cupboard without a lock. On a side shelf was a box of shells for a sawed-off shotgun, the only modern piece in the gun rack. There was a muzzle loading flintlock without rifling in the barrel such as he had first been issued when he joined the C. S. Army and a chain with sixteen leg irons which had probably been used for transporting slave coffles before the war. He took the padlock from the coffle chain, tested the hasp, and locked the armory, dropping the key in his pocket. He decided to keep the cupboard locked. The shotgun would be immobilized for Tuesday's operation, and the rest of the equipment might be of value to a museum.

Piled high on a corner of the sheriff's desk, the wanted posters were covered with dust, the bottom ones yellowed with age. Sheriff Faust had not looked at the circulars for years, but Ian was interested in the law's comments on his friends. He riffled through the top layer and tossed three of the first ten posters into the wastebasket. They were badly in need of updating.

Billy the Kid had been killed by Pat Garrett down in Mexico, Joe Burke lay in the Tombstone, Arizona, boothill. Ian himself had killed Frank Casper in Mexico, when Frank paid Ian's favorite girl an extra peso for her services. Casper's death was not officially known since the *rurales* were lax about records; but it would become officially known as soon as Ian was deputized, so he tossed Casper into the wastebasket.

In the second segment he lifted from the pile, he found one he tore up in a sudden spasm of anger.

WANTED—$50 REWARD

Ian McCleod, alias Johnny Loco. Gray eyes, sandy hair, medium weight, medium height, medium build. This man's nondescript appearance makes him hard to identify. The alias, Loco, was given to him because in playing poker he always draws to an inside straight. Wanted for questioning in several petty thefts and for the murder of his accomplice, Jesus Garcia, a Mexican vagrant.

The poster went as far wrong as it could go. His last name was not spelled right, and he was called Loco because he killed any man who fooled around with his women. Colonel Blicket, with the sergeant, had killed Hey You Garcia—his first name was not spelled right either—and their holdup of a cavalry train guarding the Army payroll had not been petty theft. After the heist and before they split—Ian to decoy the horse soldiers up a draw—Hey You reckoned the pouch he carried contained over $6,000 in greenbacks.

The colonel had taken Ian's cash and the law his credit.

Ian was still riled when he came across a poster which charged him with greater anger.

$5,000 REWARD—DEAD OR ALIVE

Jasper Blicket, alias the Colonel, alias Rawhead. Wanted for murder, robbery, horse theft, arson, rape and pillage. Approximately 6'6" tall. Weighs about 170. Very skinny. Completely bald. Black eyes sunk deep in sockets. Teeth shows when he grins. Former colonel in Quantrill's

Guerrillas, he plans and executes his forays in a military manner while wearing the uniform of a colonel, C.S.A. Rides a giant gray. (See Morley, Joe)

Ian smiled an ironic smile as he riffled through the posters, looking for Morley, Joe. A man worth $50 himself was soon going to kill a man whose official value was ten times as much.

$3,000 REWARD—DEAD OR ALIVE

Joe Morley, alias The Sergeant, alias the Monk. Wanted for murder, robbery, horse theft. Short, 5'5", broad, with low, sloping forehead and sloping shoulders. Hair black, almost kinky, and close cropped. Extremely long arms and short legs. No visible neck. Member of Colonel Jasper Blicket's gang. Wears Confederate kepi with sergeant's chevrons.

Ian filed the live posters in the cabinet except for those of Blicket and The Sergeant which he took to the front of the building and nailed on the wall next to the ordinance forbidding the discharge of firearms inside the town limits. Ian considered his act an idle gesture of goodwill toward a town which entrusted him with office. He did not know that within him another was laying longer-ranged plans.

Ian's pounding awakened the sheriff, who came into the office hitching his galluses. He took a leather-bound Bible out of his desk and a tin star.

"Hold up your right hand. . . . You swear to uphold the laws of Shoshone Flats? Say, 'I do.' "

"I do."

"This is your'n," Faust said, tossing the star across to Ian. "Pin it on and go over to Abe Bernbaum's to get measured for a suit. I got to go down to Bain's. He got in a shipment of beer late Saturday. It's got that skunky smell, but it's beer."

Feeling he should show an interest in his job, Ian asked,

"What's the crime situation around here, sheriff?"

"I ain't made an arrest in six weeks. Biggest trouble comes from stray Indians getting drunk and pilfering from clotheslines, stealing pigs, and such. Them Indians just don't grasp property rights. But they won't be giving us trouble much longer. Government's rounding them up and sticking them on a reservation southeast of here. Mormons don't give us no trouble. They don't smoke, drink, or cuss. Some say it's their religion. I say it's because they got so many young'uns they can't afford to smoke and drink and don't have time to cuss.

"If some Gentile steps on their toes, the Mormons don't bother us. They go straight to the Gentile. Got their own law enforcement, Bryce Peyton and his Avenging Angels. You already got trouble with Bryce over Billy, but Billy's the worst of a passel of Peyton's children, so the old man might let you off with just a horsewhipping. Course, now you're a lawman, he might want to set an example and string you up. A Gentile lawman would make a better example than a Gentile clodbuster.

"Most of my trouble, next to Indians, comes from young Gentile galoots getting drunk and getting into fights. Last week Jackie Cannon kicked Hal Murad in the mouth during a fight at Bain's saloon. Hal lost six teeth and been eating soup ever since. Good thing Jackie's a farmer. If he'd been wearing a cowpoke's pointed boots, Hal would have lost his eyeteeth.

"Don't never arrest anybody in Bain's place. It's bad for his business, and he's the biggest taxpayer in town. Besides, he gives me free beer.

"Reckon that just about covers the crime situation. I'll mosey on over to the barroom and get my breakfast beer. Would ask you along, but I know you done took the pledge."

"What do you want done around the jailhouse, sheriff?"

"Just keep the place swept out and the wanted posters filed. Ain't many set duties. Once a month, we ride shotgun for the Territorial Stage Lines from Wind River to here when the stage is hauling the payroll for the Old Hickory Mine, up near Jackson City. The Jackson City deputy picks it up here and rides it on in.

Since our run lasts from sunset to breakfast, the stage line pays us fifty cents for the night's work."

Ian became alert at the mention of a payroll. "When's our next run?"

"About three weeks or a little longer." Faust glanced at a wall calendar. "Next run's November third."

The being inside stored the information as Ian asked, "After I get measured, can I borrow your nag to ride up to Hendricks' horse ranch? The mayor said I could pick up a horse."

"Sure, son. But you don't need to bring my horse back. Long as you're taking over the riding duties, I'll be handling the administrative work, and there's no place around here I want to go to that I can't walk. What horse are you getting?"

"The one Hendricks calls Midnight."

"Well," the sheriff said, scratching the stubble on his chin, "if you're riding Midnight, might be a good idea not to get measured up for that suit. No use wasting Abe's time, and the clothes you got on are good enough to get buried in. . . . Well, I'll be seeing you, deputy, but I don't think you'll be seeing me."

Faust was sidling toward the door as he bade Ian farewell. Outside, he made a casual beeline toward Bain's saloon.

Ignoring the high sheriff's advice, Ian closed the jailhouse and walked five buildings down the boardwalk to Abe Bernbaum's tailor shop. He almost felt compassion when he entered to find the little man with the big head sitting on his heels atop a high stool, bent under his load of care, sewing a seam in a cloth he had stretched over his widespread knees.

At Ian's entrance, Abe did not move his body but swiveled his head and turned his face to his visitor. His eyes held no welcome for a potential customer, and only sadness was in his low-pitched voice. "So, Mr. McCloud, you are the new deputy? To you, who are about to die, greetings."

"Faust sent me over to get measured for my official suit."

"Black, the color of death. Always I am sewing black."

"Yes, sir," Ian said, trying to fall in with the mood of the tailor. "I intend to wear it to a lot of funerals."

"Yes," the tailor agreed, "there will be many funerals when the Avenging Angels sweep down on Shoshone Flats."

"At least six, Mr. Bernbaum"—Ian tried to cheer the man—"which ought to give you a lot of business making shrouds."

"No"—Mr. Bernbaum looked dolefully at Ian, his pushing and pulling fingers never missing a stitch—"for Abraham Bernbaum will be numbered with the Gentile dead."

"But Brother Winchester told me you were a Hebrew."

"To the Gentiles I am a Hebrew. To the Mormons I am a Gentile. Either way, Abraham Bernbaum loses."

His fingers had reached the end of the seam and they stopped. Bernbaum laid the cloth aside reverently, but gazed down on it with reproach, saying, "Always, you are black."

Straightening his legs, the tailor swung to the floor, pulling a tape measure from his pocket. Suddenly he was all briskness and business. Eyeing Ian's legs, he snapped out a length of the tape and said, "Stand flatfooted, feet six inches apart, and look straight ahead."

Ian complied, and the tailor bent to his task humming "Eli, Eli" as he worked.

"Take off your gun belt," he said, rising, "but keep your pistol in your hand. If Bryce Peyton passes the door, shoot him."

"What does he look like?" Ian asked, as the tailor measured his waist.

"A dybbuk in blue jeans, but he wears a black coat and hat on official business. Always, he smiles. Before and after, he smiles. . . . Inhale! Exhale! Such expansion. . . . That is all. May your life be long—at least six months—and your children many."

"Why the time limit on my life?"

"Two dollars a month is deducted from your salary until the suit is paid for, and the suit costs twelve dollars. If you die before, I have only salvage rights. It is my contract."

"You ever lose on them contracts?"

"On the last three deputies, I lost eight dollars. Of course, I make a little on their cerement. Not much, but it is a living."

"When will my suit be ready?"

"Not until after the saints ride. If you are killed before I deliver, I can sell the suit as new and charge extra for the alterations."

Feeling a sudden urge to ingratiate himself with the little man, Ian said, "I was sort of hoping I could get it early Tuesday morning, to be laid out in, so if I don't get it by Tuesday it won't make much difference when. . . . Mr. Winchester tells me you might know what the Angel Gabriel's name means in Hebrew."

" 'Gabriel' means 'messenger of God,' but whether it's Hebrew or Arabic I don't know. Gabriel is an angel to Muhammadans, Jews, and Christians."

"Would the meaning come from the name or the name from the meaning?"

"Such an intelligent question. I must think."

Ian himself was slightly amazed at his question. It was not the sort of question he usually asked.

"Ah, the name would come from its meaning," Bernbaum finally said, "for that is the way of language. The meaning of a thing comes first. . . . Think well on angels, young man. It is written, man is born unto trouble as the sparks fly upward. His days are swifter than the weaver's shuttle and are spent without hope."

Standing in front of Mr. Bernbaum, listening to his voice, made Ian feel like the Wailing Wall in Jerusalem, but it occurred to him that a man so expert at passing out bad news would make a natural-born justice of the peace.

"I thank you, Mr. Bernbaum, but cheer up. Maybe I can throw some business your way tomorrow. Maybe saints like to be buried in white, and six shrouds for six saints will give you a lot of white cloth to sew on."

Bernbaum did not smile, but his mien lightened with a lesser sadness. He raised his right hand in farewell as he hopped back onto the stool and intoned, *"Ave atque vale."*

"So long," Ian said as he walked out.

He liked the little man because Bernbaum made him feel happy in comparison, but it was high falutin of Abe to wish him good-bye in Hebrew.

Riding the sheriff's nag north on the Jackson Hole pike, Ian forced the horse to canter by applying spurs every ten yards, but it took him better than an hour to ride the ten miles to Hendricks' spread. When he pulled up before the ranch house, Hendricks came around the corner from the corrals in the rear. The man was bleeding slightly from a cut over his eye incurred in his morning's bronc-busting chores, but he was much more erect than he had been yesterday.

When Ian remarked on his uprightness, Hendricks explained, "This morning I got thrown backwards up against a corral bar. Kinda straightened out my hump."

Ian explained the disposition of the sheriff's horse, and Hendricks nodded. "I'll just plant the nag back into the same hole I dug it out of. . . . You ready for Midnight, son?"

"Yes, sir. If Midnight's ready for me."

"Midnight's always ready. But ma and me were fixing to have a bite. Want to come in and join us for your last dinner?"

"Long as it's not chicken," Ian said.

"Stew beef and corn pone," Hendricks said. "Chicken ain't heavy enough to hold a man down. Every ounce helps when you ride Midnight."

Ian might have enjoyed the meal more if Mrs. Hendricks' before-dinner grace had been shorter. Informed of Ian's purpose in coming to the ranch, Mrs. Hendricks prayed for his survival briefly and spent more time asking for mercy on his soul if he were tramped under the hooves of the stallion. Despite her quavering invocations in his behalf, Ian had the strong feeling that she was pulling for the horse.

After dinner, Hendricks led Ian back to the corrals, explaining, "Had to build a special pen for Midnight, one fourteen feet high. He can clear twelve feet from a standing start."

Between the plankings, Ian could glimpse the stallion, and

the peek was unsettling. It would have taken a better mathematician than Ian to estimate how many hands high the beast stood, but it was the biggest, blackest brute Ian had ever seen. When they climbed the top bar and looked down, he was awed.

"So that's the pinwheeler?"

Tossing its head and snorting, the stallion paced a restless circle inside the fence. At times it paused to paw the ground as if checking to find the hardest spots.

"Has this horse ever been rode?" Ian asked.

"Not yet," Hendricks said. "I hired a saddle tramp to break him for a hundred dollars, but the horse threw him and tromped him to death. Brought in an expert from Cheyenne who was willing to break him for three hundred dollars. The broncbuster could ride. Horse couldn't throw him, so it pinwheeled and crushed him flatter'n a pancake. I calculate the horse saved me four hundred dollars. Then I tried him, but he threw me, too."

"Why didn't he stomp you to death?"

"I was lucky. He threw me plumb out of the corral. Cleared the fourteen-foot fence by seven feet. Landed on my right shoulder. Didn't hurt me much, but really smashed my shoulder. . . . You still willing to try the horse, boy?"

"That's what I come for."

"You can back out. Take the sheriff's horse if he don't want it."

"I'd rather get the dying over with quick. Riding the sheriff's horse back to town, I might get caught by winter and die in a blizzard. I'll ride the black."

"Got any last requests?"

"Right now, I'd like about six brood mares, in season, in there with him," Ian said slowly, "but seeing as that ain't likely, just get me a saddle with an eight-inch nail drove about three inches through the cantle and a quirt with a loaded handle."

"Brother Ian, you don't want to get that horse riled by

pricking it with no nail. It's mad, right now. It might get angry, and that horse's got spirit."

"My last request, Mr. Hendricks, bring me my nail and my saddle."

As Ian hammered the nail through the rear lip of the saddle, leaving five inches extending above the leather, Hendricks lassoed the brute and tugged it, head first, into the saddling chute. When Ian cinched the saddle with all of his strength, the point of the nail protruding through the cantle touched lightly the back of the horse.

Hendricks had wrestled on the bridle and bit while Ian finished the saddling, and, champing at the bit, the horse stood finally accoutred for a combat it was eager to begin.

Hendricks handed Ian a lead-loaded quirt and said, "I sure hope I ain't lost my touch when it comes to matching man and beast, because this horse is a killer. If I've failed, Brother Ian, I'll be seeing you later in front of that radiant throne Brother Winchester preaches about, if they provide us with blinders up there."

"There's a tailor down in Shoshone Flats I'd like you to meet," Ian remarked as he swung from the top rail onto the saddle. "You and him got a lot in common."

Ian's weight in the saddle caused the nail to prick the beast, which lunged into the front of the chute with such force it knocked itself backwards. Yet it still had presence of mind enough to kick backwards at Hendricks who had jumped down to swing open the chute gate. Groggy, it shook its head before it reared and swirled into the arena, giving Ian just enough time to set his boot heels in the stirrups.

With the confidence of the unbeaten, the stallion leaped straight up, its hooves clearing the ground by four feet, and it twisted to the right as it fell back to the ground. From skull to tailbone, Ian felt the jolt in each joint of his spine when the horse landed, and to the jolt was added the agony of the clockwise torque the beast gained from its right-hand twist. But Ian's spine held, and he flailed the horse's head in vicious chops, some above the right eye, some above the left, with the loaded end of the quirt.

Again the horse soared and twisted, this time to the left, at the apogee of its orbit, giving a counterclockwise twist to its landing jolt. Again Ian's spine held. He continued to flail the brute above its eyes.

Midnight did not take kindly to the punishment. Lowering farther on its haunches, on the third leap the stallion tried for and reached a new altitude record for horses, but the altitude was sought for another purpose. Midnight gained the height to give himself time to lock his knee joints for a stiff-legged, four-point landing, with none of the shock absorbed by its own legs. Ian had time to lean forward and brace his stomach muscles for the impact, but the shock drove his chin into the saddle horn. His jawbone held. He retained consciousness even though his teeth ached and his ears rang.

Midnight had tested the rider with a few opening sashays. Now the stallion began to buck. It leaped and arched its back with the snap of a whip crack. Since this was a no-holds-barred contest and not a rodeo demonstration, Ian grabbed the saddle horn and hung on, praying the belly cinch would hold.

The cinch held, but the arch pricked the horse's back against the nail point, and Midnight got angry. When Ian, his eyes focused dead ahead, felt the muscles of the horse bunching beneath him for a supreme effort, he sensed what was coming and tensed his own leg muscles.

Midnight exploded.

This leap would have cleared the top bar of the corral on the horizontal. Still keeping his eyes level, Ian saw the horizon tilt downward, saw the clouds rushing toward him, and he knew: Midnight was pinwheeling. In its murderous yet crafty fury, the horse intended to fall on its rider and crush the man beneath it like a gnat under a sledgehammer. As the stallion soared upwards and slowly cartwheeled backwards, Ian flung himself from the saddle and stood aside, crouched, waiting for the great beast to plummet to earth.

Midnight did not fall on its rider. Instead, the horse landed with an earthshaking "whomp" on an eight-inch nail.

Neighing its agony, the beast scrambled to his haunches, blood streaming into its eyes, its forelegs slashing blindly for its unseen tormentor, but its tormentor was back in the saddle. Knowing he rode a horse which would never pinwheel again, Ian drove the lesson home, still further, by pounding the nail's head with the butt of the quirt.

The next thirty minutes of bucking grew progressively weaker. The horse was blinded by its own blood. The saddle was cinched firmly to its belly and nailed to its backbone. As Midnight's efforts eased off, Ian changed ends with the quirt, whipping the horse's rump. In the last stages, he used only spurs.

Finally the bucking died into an exhausted quivering, and Midnight, mastered at last, stood beneath him merely shaking. To impress the beast with his magnanimity, Ian gently pried the nail from its spine and leaned forward to stroke and pat its neck.

Midnight whinnied in gratitude.

So, after winning the first fall, Ian took the decision, and Hendricks opened the corral gate, shaking his head with admiration. But Midnight, gentled only for Ian, still had character. As it trotted through the gate, the horse lunged and bit Hendricks on the lump of his right shoulder.

"Didn't I tell you, McCloud," the horse breeder shrieked in pain and pride, "that horse has spirit!"

Spirit and endurance, Ian found, even as he cantered down the lane toward the pike. Tired from its breaking in, the stallion set no new marks for a furlong, but it moved with a gigantic stride. As it galloped on the run into town, Midnight set a pace for the entire ten miles only one horse in the world could have beaten—Colonel Jasper Blicket's giant gray, Traveler II.

Not only did these beings inflict pain on members of their own species, G-7 observed, they used cruelty as a policy with brutes more powerful than they; but the laughter of Hendricks when bitten by the horse suggested that they might take pleasure or pride in the pain they withstood. As a policy, G-7 had to accept Ian's cruelty toward the horse on the basis of results obtained. All the tremendous chemicoelectrical energy of the horse, which moments before had been directed toward the destruction of its rider, now flowed joyously to serve the man's ends. To the extent that G-7 could experience confusion, it was confused.

On its home planet, G-7 had been taught that kindness was the first virtue of the teacher, that patient gentleness was the shortest path for leading primitive organisms to the light, that the best training device was reward for achievement. Ian McCloud had demonstrated the probability that such preachments against violence might well be poppycock. Despite the precepts of G-7's possibly effete ancestors, fear was a spur by which the wild spirit could be goaded to correct behavior.

G-7 would have to rearrange its priorities. Extreme respect for energy systems might prove to be an excess of piety on a planet where energy abounded and host organisms were so perverse. Already Ian was using his synapses for connections G-7 had not foreseen.

The nail in the saddle had been all Ian's idea, and the man had understood the nature of the horse with an understanding more sutble than G-7's. Indeed the horse was a spirited brute, but no more spirited than the brute astride it, and G-7 reveled in the power of the host it had chosen.

G-7 realized its pride in Ian's power was a spiritual weakness, but the logic of the situation supported its pride. Sainthood was never a calling for ribbon clerks. Sainthood demanded the reckless courage of one who would draw to an inside straight, and Ian McCloud was its man. If McCloud chose to cudgel discipline into his fellow brutes, the true function of G-7 then would be to ameliorate the blows and trust that somehow good would be the final goal of ill.

Complacent in its pride and slothful in its ease, G-7 relaxed its tendrils along Ian's neural paths, feeling the wind on Ian's face, hearing the windrush in his ears, and thrilling to the undulating glide of the stallion. Occasionally, playfully, it fluttered a tendril in a certain area of Ian's brain to tease out memories of watermelons.

This planet, Earth, was shaping into a garden of earthly delights to equal Vulvula.

5

THREE P.M., Tuesday.

To Ian even the sunlight along the street of the empty town seemed lonely as he went from door to door, testing locks. His boot heels clumped hollowly along the boardwalk, and the clop-clop of Midnight's hooves echoed his footfalls with a ghostly sound as the horse, like a faithful dog, followed its master down the boardwalk.

Ian was paying his last respects to the town which had befriended him. Checking the lock on the tailor's shop almost created in Ian an attack of nostalgia. Abe Bernbaum—there was a man who could appreciate melancholy. Ian's greatest regret in leaving Shoshone Flats came from his knowledge that he would not die here. Nothing would have pleased his corpse more than to have Abe as its chief pallbearer.

His footsteps quickened and his heart lightened as Ian walked from the shadow of Bernbaum's shop and crossed the street toward the door of the bank kept open by provisions of its territorial charter.

He looped the reins of Midnight over the hitching rack to prevent the horse from following him inside and strode into the bank. Loosening his pistol in ils holster, he walked into the dark interior, his eyes adjusting to the change of light as he neared the teller's cage.

Knees spread, seated on his heels atop his high stool, a coat of black broadcloth spread over his kneecaps, Abe Bernbaum was acting as teller and sewing buttonholes.

"What are you doing here?"

"Acting as moneychanger for the Christians. Some Mormon might ride in to pay on a note."

"Why ain't you at the picnic?"

"I cannot forsake Israel for a ham sandwich. But if you're going to stay in town, you can watch the bank and I'll go to the picnic. It is my wish to be as far from you as I can get when the Avenging Angels ride. Though it is written that man who is born of woman has but a little while to suffer, I see no point in cutting short my allotted suffering time."

Since Abe had not looked up and apparently did not intend to, Ian saw no point in threatening him with a drawn pistol.

"Abe, I want all the money in the bank's safe."

Fingers flicking, Abe said, "Get it yourself, deputy. The safe's not locked. But, as town official, you're required to sign for all withdrawals."

This was proving fair to be the most unusual holdup he had ever pulled, Ian thought, as he opened the cage door and walked back to the safe. He opened it and pulled out the money drawer. A glance told him the drawer contained only a ten, two fives, three ones, and some loose change.

"Is this all the money in the kitty?" he called over to Abe.

"Twenty-three dollars and thirty-two cents," Abe said. "On Saturday the payroll must be met. Eleven dollars and fifty cents to you, twelve dollars and twenty cents to the high sheriff, and fifty cents for me. Someone is going to be asked to accept scrip, and it will not be a Methodist Gentile." His voice sunk low in despair. "It will be this Jewish Gentile."

"I've seen lots more money in a poker pot," Ian said in disgust.

"Not in Shoshone Flats you didn't. Poker playing is outlawed by the city ordinance against gambling."

"Is this all tax money?"

"Yes."

"Who collects the taxes?"

"Mayor Winchester."

"Who pays the taxes?"

"Mr. Bain. The mayor does not approve of drinking, so the saloon is taxed and taxed and taxed."

"Don't the people around here keep their money in the bank?"

"Not yet."

"Not yet," Ian echoed in astonishment. "Is there a season for banking around here?"

"Weather's a part of it. Few Mormons deposit here, for in bad weather they can't get to town. If you should open the road, as Mayor Winchester promised, perhaps more Mormons would come. But mostly the people have no confidence in the law's protection. Myself, I could rob the bank and outrun Sheriff Faust on foot, but the money would not pay me for the footrace."

"How long do you figure it would take for the people to put their money in the bank if they could rely on the law?"

Abe lifted his eyes and spoke with quiet assurance.

"For me, after today—if Deputy McCloud should live so long. If you survive this day, you should live forever. By now, Bryce Peyton has conferred with his bright angel, Moroni, gotten his instructions, and six black saints are riding . . . riding . . . riding."

As Abe's voice dwindled into a sinister and ominous silence, its dramatic effect was lost on Ian whose thoughts skittered off at an obtuse angle.

"I heard tell Peyton could hear voices," he remarked, as he walked out of the cage, leaving the money behind. "I didn't know whose. This Moroni's a new angel on me."

He leaned against the teller's window, thoughtfully pounding his fist into his palm, remembering the thought he had had last week: Either quit playing poker or find richer banks to rob. He had no choice of banks in Shoshone Flats, but this one could be made a lot richer with patience and planning.

Plan ahead, Colonel Blicket had always told him back in the palmy days of their relationship. Standing here now, Ian remembered the injunction and planned.

In three weeks, the stage would haul the payroll from Wind River to the mine. If, by then, he had proved that a strong lawman could enforce law and order in Shoshone Flats and had built an all-weather road to lure the Mormons into town, trusting depositors would swell the coffers of the bank. As a respected deputy, he could ride shotgun for the stagecoach of the Wind River to Shoshone Flats leg of the journey, hold up the stage en route, ride into town, and knock off the bank.

The mine's payroll and the bank might provide the biggest haul since the James boys hit Richfield, Minnesota. Johnny Loco, an ordinary run-of-the-road gunslinger with a mere $50 bounty on his head, might go down in history by setting a record for a one man heist. It was a distinction worth waiting for.

But he'd have to get the road built by September 3, the day the payroll was hauled, and the town needed a labor force and money for the road fund, right now. There wasn't enough money in the bank to furnish him with the ante to try for a road fund at the poker tables, even if he could play poker.

Play poker! That was a solution.

He turned to Abe, talking fast, "Abe, I'm going to make an official visit to the picnic. Somebody's got to make Christians out of them Mormons, and it might as well be me. How long will it take you to finish my suit?"

"Ordinarily it would take two hours. If you're going to wait here for it, it'll take fifteen minutes."

"Abe, I'll see that you're paid in full for that suit on my first payday, plus a bonus, if you'll do me a favor."

"What collateral could you possibly offer?"

"You don't do me the favor till tomorrow. If I'm killed, you're only out of the use of the suit for one afternoon."

"Name your favor, deputy."

"Accept an appointment as justice of the peace at eight o'clock tomorrow morning."

"Ian, I'm no judge," Bernbaum exploded. "The only law I know is the law handed down by Moses, and I observe that it does not apply in Shoshone Flats."

"Abe, if the law of Moses was good enough for Jesus Christ, it's good enough for Ian McCloud. This is how it will work. I'll put a defendant in front of you, and you give him ten days or ten dollars unless I tug my ear. If I tug my ear, that means he's guilty, so give him twenty days or thirty dollars. I'll give you a dollar out of every ten dollars I collect."

Suddenly interested, Abe looked up. "That sounds logical, ten percent of all fines as court costs."

"However it figures out. Keep sewing."

Twenty minutes later, garbed in official black, Ian was galloping south on his matching-color stallion, the town's tax problems on their way to being solved, pending the mayor's approval; the town's court set up, pending the mayor's approval of the appointment; and a schedule set which included, at the end of three weeks, the double robbery of a stagecoach with a payroll and a bank with deposits.

Ian's mind was functioning at such a peak of creativity it had begun to explore a plan to bring Colonel Blicket and The Sergeant north to get in on the killing, as victims.

Only one problem he could not solve: Where would he find and arrest twelve or fourteen able-bodied lawbreakers quickly enough to get the road started and finished by September 3?

When Ian galloped up to the picnic meadow spread along a curve in the river, he saw Gabriella surrounded by three full circles of Gentile gallants. She spotted him on the heights of Midnight and managed a fluttering wave of her handkerchief. He waved back, unable to see her face below the shoulders of all the tall young men who had come courting after Billy Peyton fell. Liza was there with two and a half circles of men surrounding her.

Ian swung from the saddle after he spotted Mr. Bain, and tethered Midnight to keep the horse from following him into the crowd and stepping on someone's toes. He cut the saloon keeper from Liza's herd, led him aside, and went straight to the point, "Mr. Bain, how'd you like to offer a little game of poker as an amusement to the customers of your place?"

"Deputy, I've wanted to do that for so long I can taste the poker chips. With only drinking to divert them, the customers are working my poor girls to their bones."

"How many tables could you set up?"

"Eight, easy. Maybe ten."

"All right. I'm going to get you poker parlor rights in Shoshone Flats. You take a dollar an hour, the house's cut, from the kitty at each table, and you play from six P.M. till two A.M. You keep fifty cents for yourself, give fifty cents to the town, and you won't be taxed anymore."

Brother Winchester took longer to cut from his group because he was surrounded by the ladies of the church. Ian finally sent Liza in, who had broken through her circle to compliment Ian on his suit and bronc-busting ability.

"They tell me *you* pinwheeled and near broke that horse's back."

Brother Winchester was solemn as they walked away from the crowd, and he listened as Ian explained his plan. He scuffed his toe against the grass and said, "Heck, Brother Ian, gambling's against my principles, as a preacher. So's whiskey, but I'd be run out of town if I tried to stop drinking."

"I can't say I don't disagree with you, Brother Winchester, but draw poker ain't gambling. It's a game of skill. You can keep the gambling laws and allow draw poker. You've got to look at this matter through the eyes of the mayor, not the preacher. I've been sounding out the folks in Shoshone Flats, and there's talk of electing a gambling mayor next June. Half of that road fund would go for your administration, and you deserve a salary for your labors. As long as the people are bound to have poker anyway, mayor, let it be done under a Christian administration, I say."

"You bring up some powerful arguments, Brother Ian. Let me walk alone to under yonder tree and ask for guidance in this matter."

"While you're checking, Reverend, ask about getting Abe Bernbaum appointed justice of the peace."

"That's my province, Brother Ian. Does Abe know the law?"

"Yes, sir."

"Then he's your J.P."

Brother Winchester must have had a direct line to heaven, Ian felt, for he was gone only slightly more than a minute. When he returned, his long face was split by a smile.

"It's all set, Deputy McCloud. Bain can have draw poker, long as it's two-card draw. Now all we need's the road gang. I got confidence you'll get one, but don't go around arresting people free-handed. We got to get them and let them know why they're got. It's got to be legal because they'll be voting, at least by next June."

Together they walked back to the picnic table, the mayor putting a fatherly arm over Ian's shoulder. "I've got my eye on you, deputy. You keep up the good work and you're going to be made high sheriff of my town. But don't arrest any Mormons. They don't vote in our elections, and I don't want them to start. So leave them good people alone lest it's a matter of life and death."

Ian appreciated the compliment even though he knew his work was just beginning and the toughest job, rounding up a work gang, lay ahead. Looking around him at the scrubbed faces of the young Gentiles, he couldn't see one that looked like a lawbreaker. Yet, wearing a black suit with a tin star, he didn't look like a lawbreaker either.

For a while Ian enjoyed the plaudits of the men who gathered around to compliment him on his horsemanship and to admire, at a safe distance, Midnight. He enjoyed, too, the comments of the ladies on his new suit as he tasted the delicacies spread out on the tables, until Liza broke away from her admirers long enough to whisper, "I've got something special for you in the back of my buggy."

He figured she meant a hamper of chicken, but before he could force a thanks to his lips, she was whisked away. Likely females were scarce in the Wyoming Territory. He hadn't managed a word with Gabriella and not more than a sentence with Liza. No wonder there was bad blood between the many-wived Mormons and the women-scarce Gentiles.

Ian was grateful for his relative solitude. He had problems to consider. The take from the poker tables would give him a highway fund and he could get a sealed bid from the general store to furnish him with wheelbarrows, graders, and shovels, but the road gang was going to be a problem. From the looks of this crowd, there were not enough Gentile lawbreakers in the valley to build a footpath. To Ian, the obvious solution would be to ride south and round up a few Mormons on bigamy charges and hold them in jail until after election day.

As he stood apart, ruminating, that which all but Ian had dreaded came to pass.

Around him the flutter of voices died on the summer air. A silence fell, broken only by the indrawn gasp of a woman standing nearby who cried, "Here come the saints!"

Ian followed her gaze southwestward and saw, on a hillock outlined against the sky, six black horses bearing six riders garbed in black. A chill wind that did not stir the air swept in from the horsemen as, riding abreast in an even rank, they walked their mounts slowly down the slope toward the meadow and the frozen crowd. Implacable, awesome, funereal, they came on.

In the silence Ian's voice sounded calm, authoritative, almost cheerful as he spoke to the Gentiles, "You folks stay to the left of the tables, away from me. None of you will get hurt if you fall to the ground when the bullets start firing. Some of theirs might not be aimed straight."

He strode a few yards to the right of the tables and forward to halt, facing the horsemen, his legs spread, his knees bent slightly. Moving as slowly as mourners, the riders came toward him. He could make out their faces now. A lanky man in the center wore a grim smile which bared his teeth. That would be the stake superintendent, Peyton.

Fifteen yards from the lone man, the procession halted, almost as one, and the man with the smile held up his arm.

"Be you Ian McCloud?" he called.

"I'm Ian McCloud, and you're likely to be Bryce Peyton, recently deceased, if one of your boys makes a sudden move. Any of your saints feel an urge to sneeze, he'd better hold it. You'll be killed first, the next five won't be around long enough to grieve."

Suddenly, from dead behind him, Liza's voice rang over Ian's shoulder. "I'm with you, Ian. That something special I brought for you is aimed and loaded for Mormon meat. I'll take the two undertakers on the right."

"Get out of the line of fire," he hissed backwards. "There ain't but six of them."

"We come in peace," Bryce Peyton called. "I come to thank you, Ian McCloud, for shooting some sense into my boy Billy's head. After you blowed off his trigger finger, he give up the idea of being a gunfighter, and he's down on the south forty now, bandaged hand and all, plowing for winter wheat. All that boy was ever good for was farming, and now he knows it."

"You're welcome," Ian called, still crouched. He was falling for no Mountain Meadows trick. These men, all six of them, had not ridden this far to thank him for straightening out some wild galoot.

"But mostly I've come, with witnesses, to speak to the father of one Gabriella Stewart. My son, Billy, wants to come courting; I want to talk dowry."

"Her pa's dead," Widow Stewart called.

Impelled by a sudden and inexplicable interest, Ian shouted across the intervening yards. "But maybe you can still talk to

80

her pa, Peyton, if he's in heaven. I hear you can talk to an angel named Moroni.''

"Nope, not Moroni," the grim but still smiling Mormon called back. "I talk to Namoo. He's my personal angel. I talked to Moroni once, but he's hard to get to. And I never heard of no angel called Stewart."

"I don't mean Stewart's an angel," Ian corrected him. "Talking direct to Stewart ain't the idea. . . . But you keep calling them angels he. Is angels boys?"

It was the craziest talk Ian had ever held over the barrel of a pistol, but the Mormon seemed interested.

"I wouldn't know, McCloud. I ain't never seen an angel with its robes off, but I just don't feel right calling an angel it like a horse or dog."

"What do angels look like?"

"Pure light, son. Robed in radiance the likes of which you never saw before."

Now Ian was less amazed by his own questions than by the alacrity with which Peyton answered them, and on the sidelines Brother Winchester joined in the discussion.

"That's what I been telling them, Superintendent Peyton. See, brothers and sisters, here's a man who knows."

"You wear blinders when you talk to angels?"

The question was hurled from the far side of the tables by Hendricks, the horse breeder, and Ian waved to the gallery for silence, calling over to Peyton, "What I mean, Mr. Peyton, is that you can ask Namoo to ask Moroni to ask Gabriel to go over and talk to Mr. Stewart. . . ."

As Ian commenced to explain to Bryce Peyton a logical solution to the Mormon's problem, commenting to himself how easy it was to solve other people's problems, Liza screamed behind him, "I'm the girl's mother, and I handle the dowries in this family. Billy can take potluck with the other boys when he comes calling, but Gabe's taking nothing with her when she leaves my bed and board but her pa's books, and that's all Billy Peyton's worth."

"Agreed, ma'am," Bryce Peyton said. "I thank you, and I'll tell Billy."

Bryce Peyton held up his hand in a gesture of farewell. Remembering that this man was a stake superintendent, Ian yelled "Why don't you light and have a bite with us super. I'd like to talk more about them angels."

"I'm mighty obliged, son, but I can't accept. I got twenty-three mouths to feed, and they keep me right busy. Maybe with Billy farming I'll have more time when crops are laid by."

Still smiling, Peyton wheeled his horse and with his five lesser saints rode back up the hill. He had smiled all through Liza's speech, and she had been downright unpleasant. Bryce Peyton had a facial affliction of some sort, Ian decided.

"All right, folks, you can go back to your socializing," Ian said. "It's all over."

He turned to Liza. "I thank you for backing me up, ma'am, but you've got to be more careful. You ought not to go risking a woman like you in Wyoming."

"No trouble at all, Ian," she said. "But me and Gabe ain't had the chance to visit with you. Why don't you ride back with us as far as the ranch on your way to town?"

"I'd be right happy to, Liza," Ian managed to answer before a tide of young middle-aged males and a sprinkling of middling young males swept between them, a few eddying around Ian to congratulate him on his stand against the Mormons.

Ian acknowledged the compliments as graciously as his preoccupation permitted, but his one remaining task, the acquisition of a road gang, oppressed his mind and led him to a sympathetic appreciation of the problems of lawmen. He had to jail enough men to build the road and he had to do it legally, without knowing the law, and he could not arrest drunks in the saloon or Mormons. By the time the town's government got through putting hedges around its law enforcer, he thought ruefully, he'd be able to arrest only bushwhackers who shot people in the back in broad daylight in the presence of at least three witnesses.

One good thing had happened today, the picnic. After riding home from a whole afternoon of eating, Liza would be in no mood to fix a chicken supper, for it was getting late. He could look forward to some uninterrupted courting time with Gabriella as long as he pastured Midnight out of hearing distance.

The horse was getting to be a mite jealous of him, and, to make it worse, the beast was a stallion.

6

SUNSET had faded to purple when the trio drew up to the widow's ranch. By the time Ian got the mare unhitched and Midnight tethered in the front pasture, Liza had lighted the lamp in the parlor and turned the wick down low.

"It's rather warmish tonight," she said. "I'll go open a few windows to cool the house. You young folks can set in the parlor, Ian, if Gabe can't bulldog you out to the porch swing. Eithe, you won't disturb me. I sleep in the back bedroom. I go to roost with the chickens since I get up with them, and after all that eating and excitement, I ought to sleep like a log."

"I'd like to set out on the front steps for a while," Ian began, "if Gabe's willing. . . ."

"She's willing."

". . . and learn something about the stars from a teacher. It beats me how I been studying about the stars and angels lately."

"Some nice things up there." Liza nodded. "Some nice things lower down, too. Well, good night, you 'uns. Don't do anything I'd do."

"Don't mind mama's language," Gabriella said, after her mother left, "because she's got a little Eve in her. Maybe more of Eve than Eve had. My mother would have never tempted

Adam with an apple; she would have baked him an apple pie."

"That was brave of her, standing behind me like she did," Ian commented. "If the Mormons had drilled me, the bullet could have hit her."

"She's bold, all right. . . . Let's go sit in the swing, Ian. It's stuffy in here."

"To tell the truth, Gabe, I'd rather set on the steps and have you name some of the stars for me."

"Come then. I'll show you the stars first."

Going onto the porch, he closed the parlor door behind him to keep from outlining himself against the light and said, "We can see the stars better in the dark."

From the far darkness of the front pasture, Midnight nickered a greeting as the horse saw its master emerge.

"That's the darnedest horse I ever did see," Ian commented. "One day it tries to kill me, the next it follows me around like a dog."

"It loves you Ian, because it knows you're a very masterful person."

Seating her on his left to keep his holster free, he looked up toward the road but couldn't see the horse in the darkness. With a horse the color of midnight, a man wouldn't be able to make a quick getaway in the dark because he'd have to spend some time looking for his horse. He wouldn't be having that trouble when he took over Colonel Blicket's Kentucky-bred gray. Only fog could hide Traveler II, and there were far fewer fogs than there were dark nights.

He felt slightly zany thinking about the gray while he sat with a girl beside him under the light of the Western stars with a faint scent of purple sage wafting in from the wastelands.

"Funny thing," he said, "I've rode under the stars all my life and never paid them no mind. Course, if I rode out some cloudless night and didn't see none up there, I'd be tolerably surprised. But ever since I met you I been thinking different. You may think me bold in telling you this, Gabriella, but maybe it's you that set me thinking about stars and angels."

"I know you're bold, Ian," she murmured, "and women love a brave man. But how in the world could I set you to thinking about things so unwordly. Is it because I'm a schoolteacher?"

"No'm," he said, thinking that she couldn't do anything more than slap his jaws if he told her the truth. "The other night, after I met you, I was looking up at the stars, and I'll be a wart-headed horned toad if the Milky Way up yonder didn't remind me of the freckles under your eyes."

"Why, Ian! That's a pretty thing to tell me. It may not be grammatical, but it sure is poetical. Now, tell me, why do I remind you of angels?"

"I reckon it's the way you walk, Gabriella, like an angel flies. I'm not saying there ain't some hefty parts to you, but even the hefty parts are heavenly."

"These steps are a little hard, Ian. The swing has pads."

Although he liked the idea of sitting in the swing with her, years of being hunted had honed his instincts, and now he sensed that something besides the horse lurked in the darkness, some other unseen listener. If he had to draw quickly, the swing would give him an unstable platform.

"First, I'd like to find out about the stars," he insisted. "Course, I guide on the North Star, but that's the only one I know by name."

"Very well, Ian. Close your right eye, lean your head over, and sight along my arm with your left eye so you can see exactly where I'm pointing."

To balance himself, he flattened his palm against the boards on the other side of her which placed his arm around her. She understood he was merely balancing himself, because she had to hang onto his left thigh with her left hand to keep her own balance as she pointed.

"The one yonder is Betelgeuse," she said, "and the big bright one is Aldebaran in the constellation Taurus. 'Taurus' means 'the bull,' and it's chasing the Seven Sisters. Looks like the bull's about to catch Merope; she's the veiled one of the

Seven Sisters and apt to be unveiled in a hurry. Now, Betelgeuse is in Orion, and Orion's a hunter. Perhaps he intends to shoot the bull and take the Seven Sisters for himself."

Listening raptly, Ian figured the Seven Sisters were in for it, one way or the other, for Gabriella's words made the stars come alive. With her as a teacher, he might have become an astrologer.

"That group near the polestar is the constellation called Andromeda, named after a woman who consorted with some strange creatures. If the whole truth were known about her, no gentleman would be caught taking that woman to church. . . ."

Gabriella hadn't seemed too interested in the stars at the outset, but she was warming up to the subject now. He couldn't remember the names of most of them—couldn't even see them since the down of her arm blocked his view—but he would not have changed places for anything in the sky. Her shoulder fit the hollow of his cheek, and her perfume was sweeter than that of the honeysuckle vine.

He had never known there were so many stars. Some names he could remember, such as Abraham Lincoln and Robert E. Lee, but he knew, after she named Andromeda, that he'd never be able to match all these stars with their names.

When, finally, she grew tired, she leaned her head against his and dropped her pointing hand into his hand. "Now, tell me, Ian. What do you want most out of life?"

At the moment, he wanted about fourteen men for a road gang, but he didn't think it proper to talk about lawbreakers to a schoolteacher.

"You tell me first," he stalled.

"I'd like a good stone schoolhouse built close to the Mormon's stake boundary with lots of students paying two dollars head tax. I'd like for about ten of my students to be by my own brave, strong husband."

"That would be about thirty dollars tuition," he said. "Maybe that's why the Mormons won't send their children to school. Mr. Bryce Peyton's eighteen would cost him about seventy dollars, likely more'n he makes for a year. If you cut your rate on big orders, maybe the Mormons would come in."

"One thing I'm bound and determined, Ian, is never to lower my fees. A dollar earned is a dollar saved, I say."

"I ain't really took to the idea myself," he admitted. "I was just practicing my sums."

"Fie on sums. Now, you tell me Ian, what would you like to do most, right now?"

Right now, he would like for her to kiss him and hug him, but he was shy around schoolteachers with high ideals, so he merely said, "You'd slap my face if I told you."

"You know I'm dead set against violence. Go right ahead and tell me."

"Ladies first."

"Cross your heart and hope to die if you tell?"

"Cross my heart," he promised.

"I'd like to have one good, solid sin under my belt," she confessed, "so I could go up to the altar and confess it in church. I feel a might lonely, sitting back there in the pews all by myself when the other women go strutting up. Then mama won't lord it over me. Tell me, Ian, have you ever had a hankering to sin?"

"Not till right now, Gabe. All other times, I just fall into them, natural like. But I'd like to march up to the altar and kneel beside you."

"Why, Ian, that's the nicest thing a boy ever said to me. I want to reward you with something that almost any girl can give a boy, but it counts for more when it's give for the first time. I want to give you the first kiss I ever gave a boy."

"I'd really appreciate it, Gabe."

She reached up and kissed him on the lips, but she didn't hug him.

"That's half of what I wanted," he admitted, "but it looks like I'm going to have to take the other half on my own."

He put his arms around her and hugged her, giving her back a kiss.

"To the swing, Ian," she whispered.

Now he knew what Bain had meant when the saloon keeper said he could taste poker chips. Ian could taste the wood, paint, cushions, and chain the swing swung by, and he was going to chance it if it meant getting gunned down in the dark.

"Let's go, girl."

As he stood, he could faintly see from the corner of his eyes a deeper darkness move behind the dark honeysuckle vines on the south side of the porch. "Gabe, we got us a snooper," he whispered, and sprinted along the yard toward the vines, drawing his pistol.

He was running in high-heeled boots, and he had to swing around a rosebush planted near the corner of the porch. Whoever it had been was alerted by Ian's movement and was sprinting toward the ravine. Ian pulled to a halt, knowing he was beaten before he started, for the whop-whop of shoes hitting the ground was dwindling across the side yard.

Probably some chicken-stealing Indian, Ian decided; the snooper was running too fast to be a white man.

Suddenly the rapid whop-whop of the running shoes ended in a sodden whomp, and there was silence.

"Some Indian's necked himself on the clothesline, Gabe," he called to the girl, keeping his voice low. "Crack the parlor door to give us a little light, but go easy so you don't wake up your mama. She'd die if she thought some Indian was stealing her chickens."

He walked through the dark to the clothesline and felt along it until he stepped on a body. Grabbing it by a leg, he dragged it toward the front porch. From its weight, it might make a good culvert digger, except Indians were lazy. Gabriella watched from the porch as he dragged the body into the spreading sliver of light from the parlor.

His Indian was Billy Peyton, bandaged hand and all, dressed in overall and shod in clodknockers. In a fit of rage, Ian drew back his foot and kicked the supine farmer prone.

Peyton's rib cracked, he moaned, and Gabriella screamed from the porch, "Don't do that, Ian. Oh, please don't!"

89

Denied physical expression by the girl's dislike of violence, Ian shouted down at Peyton, "Come on, act alive. I heard you moan, so I know you ain't dead. So far, all you've got is a little necking. I know you've took more than this."

Suddenly Liza's voice keened through the front bedroom window, "Gentle does it, Ian. That filly ain't been broke yet."

"Oh, mother," Gabriella shouted. "Get back to your own bedroom and quit eavesdropping."

As Gabriella rushed over to slam the window shut, Billy Peyson sat up, rubbing his jaw.

"Why are you sneaking around here, plowboy?" Ian asked.

"I brought over your laundry, Mr. McCloud, like you told me to do."

He reached into his back pocket and pulled out Ian's bandanna, freshly laundered, starched, and ironed. "I didn't want to take it all the way to town. I'm a little sensitive about my finger, and farming's been keeping me busy. Besides, I wanted to see if Miss Stewart would let me call on her when you're not visiting, because I know she wants them Mormon children for her school and I can help."

"Billy Peyton, you can call on me if you wish, but I'll never marry a Mormon."

"I've decided to convert, ma'am. I'm joining the Methodist Church next Sunday, and I'd be powerfully pleased if you'd let me come calling, if you're not ashamed to be seen with a cripple like me."

"Oh, hush up, Billy. You're no cripple. Quit feeling sorry for yourself. And I'll believe you're converted when I see you baptized, next Sunday morning."

"Where's your horse?" Ian asked.

"I left my mule down in the ravine—the beast has a fondness for willow leaves—and came up on foot. I wasn't going to stay, but I got interested in the stars. Then I waited to see if you could persuade Miss Stewart to sit in the swing. I courted her for six months and never got her out of the parlor."

"Well, boy, you've brung my laundry, and you've seen all

you're going to see. Scratch gravel!"

Holding his neck, Billy Peyton stumbled off into the darkness. Listening to his footsteps make a wide circuit of the clothesline, Ian suddenly found the answer to his greatest problem. Already he knew enough about the town's laws to get him a road gang by morning and put enough money into the road fund to pay top prices for box lunches.

He turned to the girl. "I got official business in town, Gabe. I appreciate you telling me about the stars, and I'll miss swinging in the swing with you, but I've got to hightail it back to Shoshone Flats."

Gabriella seemed at once relieved and apprehensive after his announcement.

"I'm so upset by that jackleg Mormon I wouldn't make good company for a preacher, so I'm willing to tell you good night, but I don't know what I'm going to tell mama. She thinks you were yelling at me and not at Billy."

"Tell her I'll need fourteen box lunches a quarter-mile west of Dead Man's Curve at noon tomorrow. Tell her she's been appointed commissary steward for the town's jail. At the restaurant, you figure on fourteen extra hands for breakfast and supper. Charge them an extra nickel for me—because they'll dirty up your place with road dust."

Ian was withdrawing from the porch as he issued the instructions, and, turning, he moved toward Midnight with swift, purposeful strides. The stallion must have sensed the inner urgency of the master who swung aboard it, for it swallowed the darkness in giant gulps as it raced northward toward Shoshone Flats.

G-7 was foiled again.

Granted its host was responding to short-range objectives designed to lead a man of limited vision to long-range goals, McCloud was avoiding for the most trivial of reasons those diversions G-7 wished to explore for educational purposes. On the porch, the girl had screwed her courage to the point where she could essay a feeble attempt at dalliance—though no hosannas could be raised for the directness of her method—yet, in the honeysuckle embalmed darkness, McCloud could not see what flowers were at his feet. This man, so direct, brutal, and effective with other men and horses, had stifled his rapacity for the weak female out of some incomprehensible desire to protect the virtue of Western womanhood.

Of what value was this virtue the man helped the girl to hoard against himself? Virginity were no treasure till spent as Liza could have told them, robust, yearning Liza. Love was not love which faltered when it altercation found. Just when G-7 began to feel in the darkness of Ian's mind the beginning glow of sunrise, the phantom radiance vanished and it was wrapped again in night, once by the idea of a nail in a saddle and now by a clothesline.

G-7 realized that it and its host were growing polarized along differing axes. While the man fumbled toward the hesitant virgin on the porch, a veritable earth mother crouched palpitant in the darkness of the front bedroom, seeking only crumbs of vicarious pleasure. Though the mother was fifteen years older than the daughter, she was only ten years older than Ian.

One decade, a mere photon in the cold light of eternity, yet the time span acted as a barrier between the male and the superbly ovulating female with a pelvic span at least a third again as wide as her daughter's, disregarding the mammae, and G-7 had no intentions of disregarding the mammae. Ian McCloud might be its host, but Liza Stewart was its woman.

Before he walked through the swinging doors, Ian knew the poker tables had already been set up in Bain's saloon. Inside, the player piano tinkled out "The Camptown Races" with a dull sound in the middle D, but the tinkle of glasses had slowed in tempo. The laughter of women had become more solicitous and strident, for now the girls had competition. Key change of all was the pleasant murmur underlying all other noises, the whirr of shuffled cards and click of tossed chips.

Entering, moving through the astringent odor of gamblers' sweat, Ian asked the first bartender, "Where's Bain?"

"In his office, first door right, at the end of the bar."

He strode the sixty-odd feet to Bain's office, past drinkers who eyed his badge with hostility, past Sheriff Faust, whose face was hidden in the foam of a schooner of beer, past six women held erect by their corsets and together by layers of makeup. He shouldered through the feminine ogles, unheeding, knowing the girls were overworked, and unwilling to add to their burdens. Only one of them, a chicken-necked, high-cheekboned, half-breed Shoshone, possessed even an approximation of youth and good looks, and Ian's appreciation was as objective as it was casual. He had been touched by too fine a madness to be drawn to fallen women; he had looked upon Gabriella by starlight.

G-7's opinion of the girls differed, particularly regarding the Shoshone. Framed by blue-black hair, her olive skin subdued the highlights of her high cheekbones, which, themselves, imparted the quality of sculpture to a head borne regally on her slender neck. She might have been an Indian princess and the others her ladies-in-waiting, for they all shared her grace of posture, a slight forward sling to their pelvises which enhanced the harmonics of their forms.

Mr. Bain was seated at his desk, a bottle of Red Dog before him, totaling a column of figures which he shoved aside when Ian entered. He arose in greeting, "Come in, deputy. Draw up a chair and have a drink of my private stock. I know you took the pledge, but what Brother Winchester don't know won't hurt him."

Bain was wasting the ritual on Ian because the deputy was already in, seated, and reaching for the bottle of whiskey.

"Keep your seat, Bain," he said, taking a drink from the bottle. "I'm here strictly on business. Coming in, I noticed all the poker tables were full."

"Yeah, but business has been slow. I filled the last ones just before you came in."

"You're lying, Bain, but it don't make no difference. I want you to fork over eighteen dollars a night for my quarter share of the road fund and have it ready prompt every morning in cash, even if a blizzard closes your dive. That way I won't have to worry about you cheating. The first morning that money ain't forthcoming, I padlock the place."

"Deputy, you're not being reasonable. Tonight was opening night. Most nights won't be so good. Besides, I got Mayor Winchester's cut to worry about, and you'll be eating into his take."

"What Winchester don't know won't hurt him," Ian reminded Bain, "but I ain't here to do your bookkeeping. Fork up my eighteen tomorrow or close. . . . Now, here's what I want done around one tonight: Pass out a free drink to each big winner and give each table's heavy loser a double of whatever he's been drinking. Is that clear?"

"Yes, sir."

"Right now I want you to come out and stand next to me while I tell your customers I'm going to abide by the policies of Sheriff Faust, far as law enforcement's concerned."

"Boss," Bain objected, "if you tell them galoots that, they won't respect you."

"I ain't asking advice. Let's go."

Bain followed him from the office. Outside, the player piano was playing "I Dream of Jennie with the Plink-Plonk Hair."

"Turn that thing off and don't turn it on again till its fixed."

As Bain hastened to turn off the piano, Ian climbed to the top of the bar and clapped his hands for attention. As he waited for the voices to die, he marveled at his own thought processes which had grasped the connection between a posted ordinance, Billy Peyton's neck, and the habitual riotousness of Westerners. It was as if someone else were doing his thinking for him.

"Folks," he announced, "I apologize for breaking into your fun, but I'd like to tell you that as deputy of this here town I intend to carry out the policies of your beloved Sheriff Faust."

Hoots and derisive laughter arose from the crowd, but the bleary-eyed Faust lifted a fresh schooner of beer to salute himself in full approval of the announcement.

Putting a hesitant, pleading smile on his face, Ian used the first Biblical quotation of his life. "I want to remind you that wine is a mocker, strong drink is raging, and whosoever is deceived thereby, is not wise."

"Amen," some wiseacre croaked.

"But I ain't here to talk about the evils of drink. I'm here to ask you boys to cooperate with the high sheriff and me to see that the town's laws get obeyed. Please don't get too drunk to set on a horse. Please don't race your horses during business hours. And for this one I'm giving you a 'pretty please': Don't fire your pistols as you ride out tonight. I get up with the chickens, so I need my sleep.

"There's just one more thing I'd like to say. Mr. Bain has kindly agreed to get the piano fixed. To celebrate, I'm inviting you to come forward and have a drink on me. . . . Put the charges on my tab, Mr. Bain. . . . Thank you, ladies and gentlemen."

A few cheers of appreciation sounded as the men gathered at the bar, but the hurrahs had a brassy ring. In the habitual ritual, some of the drinkers lifted their glasses toward the man who was trying to buy their favors, but they no longer eyed him with hostility. They sneered at him in contempt.

As Ian turned toward the door, smiling deferentially, tipping his hat to the girls, they, too, ceased to ogle him. Instead, they gazed at him with sad-eyed professional sympathy, as if he were one of their number who would soon be called upon to render services without remuneration.

7

AFTER he returned to the jailhouse, Ian set up a cot for the sheriff in the corridor at the rear of the cell block and hung a lighted lantern on the wall to guide Faust to bed. From the armory he optimistically took all sixteen leg irons and threaded them onto the coffle chain. He spread his pallet and went to the desk where he penciled a letter to Colonel Jasper Blicket.

Dear Col.

Reckon you didn't expect to here from me, Johnny Loco. After I led them bluebellies up the canyon, like you told me to, and Hey You skeedaddled South with the money, I circled back. But my horse throwed a shoe and I had to walk to the rondevoo. Hey You was there but shot dead and the money gone. Waited for you and Sarge but when you didn't come I vamoosed. I didn't kill Hey You because I didn't have no bullets left. I shot them all at the horse soldiers. I didn't steel the swag because I didn't have no horse. They was only two nails in that shoe it throwed. You ought to kill that smithy of yourn. I wondered around in the desert till I got picked up by a Navvyhoe sheep herder. His old woman took to me so I had to kill him. I took his horse and rode north to Pokotella and hired out as shotgun for the Terrytorial stage. Next month I guard the rear end out of Wind River. It leaves there at sunset, Sept. 3, for Jackson City. About dawn the stage comes off the ramparts. If the Sarge puts a bolder on the road where it narrows along the cliff I can get the driver from behind. Bring me a running horse. It's the payroll for Old Hickory Mine, all green backs and easy to carry.

> Yr. Obdt. Svt.
> J. Loco

He addressed an envelope to Colonel J. Brazewell, General Delivery, Green River, Wyoming, sealed the letter in it, and left the jailhouse, carrying a lariat in his hand, to walk diagonally north across the street to the post office. After dropping the envelope into the wall box, he tied the rope around the cornerpost of the post office porch and uncoiled the line behind him as he went across the street to the hardware store where he tied the free end of the lariat around a porch pillar and drew the line taut with a running sheepshank.

Twenty yards north of the sheriff's office and nine feet off the ground, the rope stretched across the road. Invisible in the darkness, the barrier would remain invisible until moonrise, a full hour after the saloon closed.

The implications of Ian's letter and his rope trick concerned G-7. While it complacently assumed it was leading its host step by step to righteousness, Ian was developing long-range plans for a giant leap back into lawlessness. Earlier, G-7 had formulated an optimistic progress report it intended to send to Galactic Central, but Ian's letter indicated its planned re-alignments were askew. Its plans were becoming Ian's plots; its wisdom his cunning. Even Ian's cooperation with other members of his species was proving unilateral; they cooperated with him but not he with them.

That it had chosen a forcible host G-7 still must concede, one who applied his minimal knowledge for maximal effects, but it was not enough for one to possess the qualities of a saint, one must also be saintly. Ian's drive to avenge the murder of Jesus Garcia was illogical and sinful. Being dead, Garcia could not appreciate the effort, and Ian, now, was certainly aware from the Scriptures that vengeance did not fall under his jurisdiction. Of course, Ian was moved in part by the insult from Colonel Blicket still locked in his memory nodes, but even that motivation was suspect; words were immaterial and its host was otherwise concerned only with material considerations.

September 3, G-7 realized, was the deadline for its efforts. If Ian reached the crossroad and chose the path of darkness, it would know that it had failed on earth. But it was a Legionnaire and must not fail. It had converted the raspers of Markab 5 to Galactic Brotherhood, and it would not be defeated by the humans of Sun 3. It had a tradition to uphold, and, more, it had what its host would call "an ace in the hole."

Deep within the man who now dozed fitfully on his pallet, a man who had failed often, planned a wakeful planner which had never failed.

At midnight Sheriff Faust came in, too drunk to get his key in the lock. Awakened by the fumblings, Ian let the old man through the door and told him, "Sheriff, I fixed you a cot at the end of the cellblock because I figure we'll be using all the jail's bunks tonight."

"Deputy, I ain't going back there."

"Why not?" Ian bridled, fearing Faust might be asserting his administrative authority.

"Because I've gone as far as I can go," the sheriff answered, falling forward.

Ian caught him and tossed him over a shoulder, carrying him to the rear. Before they reached the cot, the sheriff was snoring, and with each exhalation he emitted the skunky odor of green beer.

Brought fully awake by his exertions, Ian returned to the pallet, bringing the lantern with him. For a while he lay in the pale light thinking of Gabriella with weird twists and turns of thought. She was lovely and he wanted her, but she was too frail to be the wife of a bank robber. She would do better with some God-fearing farmer who owned a big spread. Billy Peyton would qualify if he converted to the Methodists. Anyone who owned a south forty must have a north forty, about one hundred and sixty acres all told, and, besides, Billy read books.

Still, despite his poor schooling, Gabriella seemed to like him. If he didn't have other plans, he might consider reading through the fourth-, fifth-, and sixth-grade primers. A man couldn't woo a schoolteacher on a third-grade education. But he had other plans.

A man could be limited by his plans, Ian realized suddenly, while there were no limits to his plans. Drowsing here, he could plan to become President of the United States—Now *there* was a till to be tapped—and plan to court Gabriella strictly for her favors. A schoolteacher would be smart enough to know that that fate, far from being worse than death, could be downright fun.

He would court her up to the evening of September 2, then tell her, just before the evening was out, he was leaving because he did not wish to interfere with her future happiness. Seeing how unselfish he was and knowing he was leaving the country, she might have a stroke of generosity. Girls were a lot more willing to be loved when they knew a man was leaving.

In the drowsy images of beginning sleep, he could see Gabriella standing on the porch and waving good-bye tearfully to the lonesome cowboy who galloped off into the sunset toward Wind River. The pathos of the scene might have aroused him to further wakefulness had he not recalled that he would be riding east and astride Midnight. The horse would not like it when Ian took over the colonel's giant gray, but Midnight had to go. Not only was the stallion black, which handicapped it for night work, but its affections were getting to be embarrassing.

So his thoughts, skittering at times to the edge of unselfishness before drawing back, grew jumbled and confused and merged into sleep.

Awakened by the thunder of hooves from the south, the direction of Bain's saloon, Ian sat upright and rubbed his eyes, reaching for the coffle chain. Once, he remembered, a schoolteacher had told him it always paid to be polite, and he was reasonably sure that she was right, that his courtesy earlier in the barroom would be rewarded. In a few seconds now, a bunch of rowdies was going to discover that a new brand of lawman had arrived in Shoshone Flats.

Punctuated by "yippees" and "yi-ays," the hoofbeats drew nearer. When the riders were abreast of the sheriff's office, a rolling barrage of pistol blasts shook the jailhouse. The sound of the hooves dwindled northward, but only after a rapid series of thuds sounded twenty yards north.

Rising, Ian carried his manacles and lantern into the night.

At the tope barrier, Ian counted seventeen lawbreakers, sitting or lying, prone or supine, across the width of the road. One man, wearing the boots and chaps of a ranch hand, was on his feet and walking in a circle. Gleaming in the lantern light, pistols were scattered on both sides of the barrier. Some of the fallen were moaning from rope burns and bruises. A few lay motionless and soundless, either dead, dead drunk, or unconscious.

Seventeen jailbirds exceeded the town's accommodations in leg irons and bunk space. One prisoner might have to sleep standing up, and the likeliest candidate seemed the circling sleepwalker.

Ian walked over to the cowboy, raised the lantern, and asked, "What's your name, prisoner?"

Never breaking his stride but scratching his head in perplexity, the cowboy made a full circle before he answered, "I give up. What is it?"

Though taking a long stroll to nowhere, the cowhand was mobile and apparently ablebodied. He would lead the coffle back to the jailhouse, Ian decided, and turned to the fallen.

Moving among them, snapping on leg irons, he threaded the chain to put the unconscious men at the end, moving forward through the moaning men and the sitters. He left the smallest, totally unconscious man unchained. When all were chained but the circling cowboy, Ian went down the line to revive the prisoners and get the chain gang moving.

His methods were direct and effective.

Standing before the first man in line, a conscious sitter, he said, "On your feet, prisoner."

Ear pulling was too tiring, Ian decided. He stood over the next prisoner and said, "Stand up, you."

When the sitter responded with a slack-mouthed grin, Ian whipped a kick to the side of his head. The man toppled, his shoulder thudding against the ground. He bobbled back to a sitting position and bounded to his feet.

Down the line, the splat and thump of the kick and the fall caught the attention of the remaining sitters who scrambled to their feet. Moving on to a facedown moaner, Ian brought the man to his feet with a kick in the ribs. All were standing now, except for three who were out cold.

The curses, cuffs, and kicks made it plain to all who heard them that the mild-mannered deputy who had earned their contempt in the saloon was fast developing into an efficient lawman. When Ian dressed ranks, they responded with alacrity. He set the lantern on the boardwalk, grabbed the wandering cowboy's leg, slapped on the last leg iron, threaded the chain through it, and snapped the padlock.

After retrieving the lantern, Ian turned back to find the most ablebodied man was not necessarily the most able. The leg iron had reversed the walker's circle and extended his radius. He was rolling up the line by pivoting the chain gang on the unconscious anchormen.

Sprinting over, Ian reversed the man's direction, let him straighten out the line, then slapped him hard across the cheek.

The man stopped, shook his head, and said, "Huh," in the manner of a man suddenly awakened.

"What's your name?" Ian barked.

"Mickey . . . Mickey O'Shea."

Ian backhanded him on the opposite cheek and asked, "Do you know me?"

"Sho," the man said. "You're Chief I.N. Black Cloud."

Ian slapped him again. "Think harder."

"Deputy Ian McCloud."

"You'll do. Were you in the army?"

"Yes, sir."

"Which one?"

"The CSA."

"You're my point. Hold this lantern as a guidon and move out to the jail after I've made a legal announcement."

Ian walked before the middle of the line, hands on hips, his tin star glinting in the lantern light.

"Y'all are under arrest on four charges: disturbing the peace, shooting off firearms inside the town limits, racing horses on the town's street during trading hours, and being too drunk to set on a horse. Your next of kin will be notified when your horses come home without you.

"Now, listen, you mules. You front ones have got to drag the back ones to jail when I give the command, but don't jerk too hard. Them convicts is public property."

He walked over and picked up the legs of the surplus drunk. Dragging the man travois fashion to the head of the line, he shouted, "Forward, march!"

Enough ex-soldiers were among them to comply with the order and get the line moving, but it was a slow route step with the tail end dragging. Ian didn't force the pace out of concern for the drunk he was dragging. The man's head was bouncing against the boardwalk with enough force to disjoint his neck, and a dead man couldn't pay a fine or help build a road.

Ian dropped his burden off in the first cell and led the point to the rear. Peeling off prisoners as he rolled back the chain, Ian stacked the unconscious men in a pile in one cell, reasoning that they wouldn't be uncomfortable. He might have a dead one or two, but he didn't have time to take an inventory because he had to go back and collect evidence of the crimes. Anyway, the corpses would keep till morning.

He walked back to the rope with a gunnysack for collecting firearms, smelling the weapons before he dropped them into the bag. Three had not been fired, possibly because the owners were too drunk to pull the triggers, and the unfired weapons presented him with a legal problem. Was an intent to disturb the peace as grave a crime as disturbing the peace?

He solved the problem on the spot by firing the weapons before he tossed them into the gunnysack.

He was rolling up the rope when he heard a low moaning farther down the street. Swinging his lantern, he walked over to find his eighteenth prisoner, an older man whose boot heel must have caught in a stirrup, dragging him a ways. The man's weapon was still in its holster, which indicated the prisoner had not intended to break the law.

But the man was old and gray, fit only to be a water boy, and he should have known better than to associate with criminals. Ian drew the man's weapon, fired it, dropped the pistol into the bag, and dragged his eighteenth prisoner to the jail by his collar. Out of deference to the possible innocence of the oldster, Ian threw him on top of the pile in the first cell.

When he returned to the pallet, it occurred to Ian that he had ordered only fourteen lunch boxes from Liza to be brought to the work site, tomorrow. He had counted on there being enough poker winners among the prisoners to collect a few fines for the road fund, and if nobody paid their fines four prisoners wouldn't eat, unless he had some dead ones back there.

Thought of the possible dead disturbed him. He had not

planned so well, after all. No arrangements had been made with Near-Sighted Charlie to rebate part of the funeral expenses to the road fund.

Its faint luminescence hidden in the light of the moon, G-7 flitted along the magnetic fields of Earth toward the spaceship among the boulders atop the crag of Dead Man's Curve. As it zoomed and swooped in easy gradients, it mulled over the report it would send to Galactic Central.

Any objective analysis of the data it had acquired would point to its immediate withdrawal from the planet, but three factors weighed against objectivity: the potential of its host organism, once converted, to become a force for good; its failure, or more accurately, the failure of McCloud to explore the motivational power of biological attraction; and, third the vague evidence of a prior visitation which it dare not mention unless it was ready to welcome a committee of visiting luminaries.

It wasn't, primarily because of the second factor, biological attraction, which, nevertheless, would have to be touched on in the report, but in a manner commensurate with G-7's missionary purposes on the planet.

G-7 arrived at the cubelike boulder, entered the compression chamber, and moved into the control room as a cloud of condensed photons capable of operating the photoelectric communications scanner. Using the preliminary scanner to compose a rough draft, G-7 phrased the first paragraph onto the screen. Since the first paragraph was merely a situation report, it went directly to the point.

G-7 to M-17 Central, Galactic Brotherhood. Primary organisms on planet hereafter called "Earth" are bipedal hydrocarbon compounds which concert electrochemical energy into mechanical force by hinged calcium compound levers. Primary communication method of earth beings is by controlled gaseous emissions. Secondary method is achieved through differing wave lengths of light, usually bllack on white. Other methods of communication are by impact, using whips, butt ends of quirts, toes of boots.

So far, so good. G-7 encapsulated the situation report and scanned in the plans section with greater care. The final, encapsulated version read:

Rudimentary brotherhood awareness of selected host is to be amplified by reinforcing the being's binary reproductive programming in condensed but increasing increments.

Translated from officialese, G-7 was announcing its intention to enhance the power of love in its host organism, a standard operating procedure for galactic scouts. Galactic Central would accept the statement without assuming any disturbance of the subject-object relationship missionary work demanded. Of course, no entity at GC had ever seen Earth women through the eyes of an Earth man. No being, there, could evaluate the lightness of Gabriella, the beckonings of Liza, or the regal slouch of the Shoshone Princess.

For a moment, G-7's fancy dallied over the image of the half-breed dance hall girl, considering an alteration of Ian's world lines to include a visit upstairs at Bain's place. Relative to the Shoshone Princess, a visit would matter little, probably not more than a dollar. Relative to G-7 it might cost a fissioned ion to swing its host into a love groove, particularly in a setting where Ian's attentions were focused on his take from the poker tables. Besides, Ian's visit upstairs might endanger the employer-employee relationship Ian had established between himself and the saloon keeper.

Wrenching itself away from earthly thoughts, G-7 concentrated on wording the delicate third paragraph of its progress report, the predictions section. Roughly, it scanned in the message it wished to convey:

The intelligence of Earth's inhabitants makes them adequate for conversion to Galactic Brotherhood, but their morality is doubtful.

Although not yet worded in the language of diplomacy, this was the substance of the message G-7 wished to convey, but the pessimism was at odds with the *esprit de corps* of the Interplanetary Exploration Legion. Too defeatist.

G-7 revised the prediction to read:

> Conversion of Earth beings held possible.
>
> G-7

That should do it. Let GC draw its own conclusions.

G-7 encapsulated the final draft, placed the three capsules into the transmission chamber, set the accelerated light-wave length, built up the booster, and pushed the transmit button that sent the micro-blip hurtling back to Central at a constant acceleration of three to the second power commencing at the speed of light.

G-7 floated into the diffusion chamber, diffused, and moved once more into the moonlight, confident that its neutral prediction would be read as optimistic at Galactic Central. As through all previous eons, with one exception, a scout had landed and the situation was well in hand.

But the one exception might well have occurred on this planet. Probably here G-3 had vanished. It must have been deetherealized through loss of entropy, because the alternative was theoretically impossible.

The impossible alternative was that G-3 had betrayed a trust.

8

COURT convened promptly at seven A.M. in the Sheriff's Office, Town of Shoshone Flats, Territory of Wyoming, the Honorable Abraham I. Bernbaum presiding. Eighteen defendants were found guilty on two counts of disturbing the peace, firing weapons inside the town's limits, and being too drunk to ride a horse. Evidence was submitted to the court by Deputy Sheriff Ian McCloud—eighteen pistols which had been fired and were identified as belonging to the defendants.

Each defendant was given the choice of thirty days at hard labor or paying a fine of thirty dollars. Six men paid their fines and were released, twelve were incarcerated. A third charge, racing horses on a commercial street during trading hours, was dropped after the deputy consulted with the mayor, as an expression of magnanimity on the part of the town's administration. Trial was witnessed by the town's mayor and the daughter of the jail's commissary stewardess.

Monies collected were disbursed to the representative of the jail's stewardess for food purchases, to the judge for court costs, to the town's administration fund, and the town's road fund. After the trial at 7:10 A.M., the prisoners were marched to Miss Stewart's Restaurant for breakfast.

Mayor Winchester joined Ian for a ceremonial breakfast paid for from the town's administration fund. Winchester was effusive in his compliments, but he slowed down long enough to ask, "When will the road be finished, deputy?"

"September 2."

When the prisoners were returned to their cells to be held until Ian procured tools and transportation for the work gang, Sheriff Faust was temporarily awakened by the clanging cell doors. "Where'd you get all them prisoners, deputy?"

"Off a trotline."

"Keep up the good work, boy, and you'll be high sheriff when I resign."

After Ian bought implements from the hardware store and rented two wagons and four mules from the livery stable, he had three dollars left to deposit in the road fund. He made a forty-eight-dollar deposit to his personal account and was complimented by Mr. Graves, the banker, for being the major depositor in the Shoshone Flats Territorial Bank.

At a gravel pit, three miles out, the prisoners disembarked to load the wagons. Under the quiet urgings of the deputy, who personally discussed work problems with each individual, the wagons were loaded swiftly. Two abreast and in cadence, the prisoners were marched the remaining distance behind the loaded wagons with implements at "shoulder arms." Work commenced one quarter-mile west of Dead Man's Curve.

Ian used what was left of the morning to whip his crew into shape. Since all were ill with hangovers, there was a tendency among the crew members to slack off as the morning wore on, but Ian counteracted the tendency with an inspirational example.

Selecting a lanky, rawboned man who was not equaling th tempo of a man ahead of him in shoveling dirt from the drainage ditch, Ian dismounted from Midnight and said, "Hey you, over here."

When the man walked over to stand slackly before him, Ian

asked, "What's your name?"

"Hank Sheldon."

"It appears to me, Hank, you're a little slow this morning. Ain't you feeling good?"

"No, captain, I truly ain't. My stomach's still riled from all the rotgut I drunk last night, and I got a splitting headache."

Ian stepped forward and backhanded the loaded end of the quirt into the man's stomach. Hank Sheldon jackknifed forward, coughing and gasping in pain. Ian waited until the gasping slowed and then tilted the man's chin up so he could look into the prisoner's eyes. "That help your stomach any, Hank?"

"Yes, sir. It sure did. Settled it right now."

"How about that head of yours?" Ian asked. "It feel all right?"

"Clear as a bell, captain. Clear as a bell."

"Good! Now get back in the ditch and use that shovel like you meant it." He raised his voice so all could hear. "We've got twenty-eight days to build this road to Shoshone Flats. Finish it on time, and I'll give every man of you two days off for good behavior. But if any man's caught soldiering on the job, I got the cure for what ails him."

Hank Sheldon stepped up his cadence to match the increased tempo of the man ahead of him. As the work moved briskly apace, Ian rode forward to survey the curve he had vowed to conquer. An outcropping of granite twenty feet high jutted for one hundred yards from the base of the hill toward the river where the channel narrowed into the defile from which Dead Man's Curve had been cut. Forty yards back from the lip of the cut there was a slight saddleback before the hill rose to its crest.

Ian had never thought of granite as stuff to be cut through. Now reality faced him, and he knew he could spend six months whittling away at the spur with picks and shovels. He could not build the road over it, for the face of the hill was too sheer, but to tunnel under it would be even more of a task.

He turned back to the crew. It was against his principles to seek advice, but he swallowed his pride and yelled, "Any of you galoots ever done any mining?"

"Mickey O'Shea, back on the grader," someone answered.

Ian remembered the name and the man. He rode back to the place where mules were pulling a heavy log back and forth across the road ahead of the crew spreading gravel, and he called to the mule driver riding the log, "Hey you, come here."

The man leaped from the log, reached down, and picked up a large, hand-sized rock.

"If you want me, deputy, you're coming after me. I ain't taking the butt end of the quirt from you or nobody else."

Ian admired the man's spirit.

"I ain't after you. I'm after your know-how. They tell me you're a miner."

"Have been, along with a couple dozen other trades."

"Put down your rock, O'Shea, and climb this hill with me. I got to order some blasting power for cutting the edge off this hill, and I don't know how much."

Mickey O'Shea followed the horse at a wary distance and looked up at the ledge. "I'm a miner, not a road builder," he said, finally, "but if you're willing to bank a little curve through the saddleback, which looks like a fault from here, I could blow a gulch through it with maybe a ton of that new-fangled stuff they call dynamite."

"Where'd you get a ton of dynamite?"

"Give me a night off, with four fast horses and a heavy buckboard, then don't ask me no questions, and I can requisition it from the explosive shack at Old Hickory Mine."

"What'll it cost?"

"Nothing. That's why I don't want you asking me no questions."

"You got a wife or sweetheart here in this valley?"

"I got both."

"Then you'll get your night off. But let's mosey up the hill to figure the cutback line."

Atop the ledge to be blasted, almost on its lip and as yet not consciously noticed by human eyes, stood a boulder shaped as a cube three feet in all dimensions. Preset for a planetary blast-off, it was G-7's spaceship, and G-7 was not ready to depart a planet where there was very much work left to be done. Tomorrow's dynamiting would bury the craft under tons of debris.

Glad to be released from heavy labor, O'Shea was happy to climb the hill. As they neared the crest, O'Shea spotted the strangely shaped boulder and brought it to Ian's conscious attention.

"Look at that rock, captain. It's an artifact, or I'll eat my boots."

"What's an artifact?"

"Something made by hand."

The two climbed to the boulder.

"I'd say it was the cornerstone of some Aztec building," O'Shea commented, "except the Aztecs didn't get this far north."

Ian thought a moment.

"The schoolmarm wants a new stone building down near the stake boundary. This would make a cornerstone."

"I could get a crowbar and lever it over the ledge," O'Shea suggested. "It'll fall to the road, and we can haul it to the building site."

"You do that, O'Shea," Ian said with surprising amiability, "and you're my foreman."

Blasting operations the following day were so successful that Ian christened the cut "O'Shea's Gap," and had the name entered on the town's records.

Within the next week the road fund built so fast from the poker proceeds that Ian was able to hire the town's tailor to make blue denim uniforms for the prisoners at such a reasonable price that Ian was able to add almost a hundred dollars to Bernbaum's bill and still save the town money. Now he was by all odds the bank's prime depositor. When Banker Graves passed him on the sidewalk in the company of Bain and the mayor, the banker's greeting was, "Good morning, Deputy McCloud, Mr. Bain, Mayor Winchester."

After Mickey O'Shea was appointed foreman of the road crew, Ian had time for other activities. O'Shea shared his boss' determination and drive to keep the work rolling on schedule, a spirit given added impetus by the mayor's announcement that there would be an official ribbon cutting on September 2 when the road reached the town's first building.

Actually the crew required little driving. After the blast from O'Shea's Gap brought them to the attention of the valley dwellers, the crew members acquired a cheering section. Equipped in uniforms, and marching and working with military precision, the road gang drew galleries of young ladies from all religious denominations, and a few with no religious or moral affiliations, who watched from gigs and horses drawn off the road. Ian did not disapprove because the girls drove the crew to super efforts.

O'Shea was the foreman and appointed his own lead men, but Ian kept the discipline in his own hands. When Liza came to Ian with the complaint that Mr. Birnie was demanding only the best portions of the chickens for his stagecoach passengers, Ian had her put the wings and necks in black boxes. If a man gave less than his maximum effort in the morning, he was black boxed when Liza brought lunches. Less than a maximum effort for the afternoon entitled the offender to a night in the cell closest to Sheriff Faust, with his snores and skunky smell, at the end of the corridor.

Straight across the valley, the wide, graveled road inched toward Shoshone Flats. Once it was past O'Shea's Gap, progress was on schedule, but progress took planning. Ian discovered a stonemason among the prisoners and sent him ahead to construct culverts of stone instead of the board troughs originally used. O'Shea himself became so fascinated by the stone work that he spent too much time with the forward crew, and Ian black boxed the foreman.

Ian was judicious in his labor practices, not from humanity but for efficiency. He attempted to allocate the tasks according to the skills and strengths of the individuals in the crew. The old man whose pistol Ian had fired and who kept insisting he was innocent of the original charge of disturbing the peace was so convincing that Ian assigned him to the comparatively easy job of water boy. Such simple gestures helped give Ian the reputation for being a just man.

Augmenting the crew was easier since Ian had developed his reading ability. He studied the town's ordinances in order to uncover the more fragile laws. There were four vacancies in a jailhouse which would squeeze in sixteen prisoners, so he was able to act on O'Shea's request for four more workmen to form a cleanup gang to go ahead of the gravel spreaders and remove debris and fill chuckholes in the road.

Ian's coup came when he pondered aloud which of two horses was the faster in the presence of the horses' owners, two young blades who had ridden into town and were loitering before the barber shop. In the ensuing conversation, one challenged the other to a quarter-mile race using the barber's pole as a finish line. Bets were freely wagered on the outcome amid a small crowd which gathered on the boardwalk to watch the finish.

Both racers lost when they were arrested for galloping their horses down Main Street during business hours, and the horses were impounded for the use of Mickey O'Shea and the stonemason.

In addition, Ian acquired two splendid physical specimens from the bettors on the boardwalk, because gambling was still illegal in the town—draw poker had been ruled a game of skill. Unfortunately one of the bettors paid the fine, leaving Ian's work gang one short for a full complement.

Ian spent little of his working day in town. Billy Peyton had laid by his winter wheat and was hanging out at Miss Stewart's Restaurant again, and Ian did not wish to cramp Billy's style. Ian knew he would bid farewell to the girl on September 2, and in one of his rare moments of unselfishness, he felt the wealthiest Methodist landowner in the valley might prove a solace to a girl with Gabriella's sharp eye for a penny. Also, he stayed out of town because Sheriff Faust bored him.

Faust was a cornucopia of knowledge relative to distilled, brewed, or fermented spirits. When he wasn't handling his administrative problems at Bain's Saloon, he sat around the office detailing various recipes for rye whiskey, corn whiskey, and beer. Ian had run a few stills in his boyhood, so he was not interested in the details of moonshining, but he would lend an ear to the beer story.

Faust had the idea that fifty acres belonging to Billy Peyton along the creek south of Widow Stewart's ranch would be good soil for growing hops. If the Methodist would sell, Sheriff Faust told Ian, Faust was willing to pay $500 for the acreage. Faust planned to retire shortly, and he dreamed of brewing his own beer in his old age, and he was so serious about his retirement plans he had drawn the design for his oast.

As a favor to the old man, and sensing an opportunity to profit, Ian had Gabriella sound Billy out about selling the fifty acres. When the answer came, an emphatic "No," Ian understood. Billy was playing his cards close to his vest with the girl, and property was the only card Billy had.

On the job, Ian kept an open ear for suggestions from the crew, but when Mickey came up with a stonemason's request that he be permitted to span a small creek half a mile ahead with a stone arch bridge, Ian thought this suggestion too fanciful. Still, the existing wooden structure was ten yards downstream from the new place Ian wished to cross because the road was being cut through a hummock the old road skirted. Since the hummock was rocky and the rocks had to be removed, Ian figured they could be used to bridge the creek, so he gave the foreman the go-ahead.

Mickey thought for a moment, and said, "The stonemason will need an assistant, captain, a big man to lift the rocks by himself."

Ian shrugged. "We got space for one more. I'll ride into town and see what I can pick up."

Within an hour after he arrived in Shoshone Flats, Ian had spotted his man, a giant almost seven feet tall and built to mammoth proportions. Ian followed his prey at a discreet distance, waiting for the man to break a law.

To Ian's disappointment, the giant walked on a straight, purposeful line from the hardware store to Abe's tailor shop, moving as if he knew where and why he was going and wasting no time. Obviously Ian was tailing a respectable citizen. Even so, he observed the length of the man's stride and the width of his shoulders with avidity. Ian wanted the giant and was determined to get him.

As Ian eased up to the doorway of the tailor's shop, his hopes arose. Inside, the giant was arguing with Bernbaum, his voice rumbling with an anger that shook the shop.

"I ain't paying no twelve fifty for the suit, Abe. I talked to a man in Pocatello who was wearing one just like it he got for eleven eight-eight."

"Yes, sir," Ian heard Abe explain, "but there is a railhead at Pocatello. The goods must be shipped, and someone must pay the freight. Also, Jebediah, a man of your size takes more cloth."

"I'll listen to reason, Abe, when you can give me a reason. All right, I take ten cents more cloth, and you pay fifteen for the hauling—that's being generous—so you add two bits to the eleven eight-eight. The way I figure, that suit shouldn't cost me more than twenty-five cents over the eleven eight-eight or, to be exact, twelve dollars and thirteen cents. I ain't paying you a penny more."

That did it. The man was a swindler. A quarter added to eleven eighty-eight came out to twelve twenty-three, as any fool knew. The big man had deliberately forgot to carry the one. And he was the worse sort of swindler, using his size to scare little Abe while he stood there juggling figures. Any citizen who'd bully a man was no better than a lawman.

"But I've finished the suit, Mr. Clayton," Abe insisted, "and we agreed, before I started, that twelve fifty was a fair price."

"That was before I sent to the city to find out I was getting slickered."

"But, Jeb, consider the fabric. Look at this seam. Feel the material! You may pay a little extra with Bernbaum, but you get a lot more. There's not a better-tailored piece of cloth in all the territory. Believe me, J. C., this suit would be a bargain at thirteen fifty."

"I'm willing to add another twelve cents for your artistic touch," the voice rumbled, "and make it an even twelve dollars and two bits."

There the man was again with his figures, and Ian figured it was time for the law to take a hand. He stepped through the doorway and into the shop, asking, "Abe, did this man agree to pay you twelve dollars and four bits for that suit?"

Abe seemed startled and upset by Ian's entrance.

"Yes, deputy. That was about the figure we agreed on."

"Looks like we got a clear case of defrauding a merchant, Abe," Ian said. "You're under arrest, mister."

"Under arrest?" The big man turned and looked down on his accuser. "Mister, me and Abe's just bargaining."

"Swindling a storekeeper ain't the kind of bargaining we take to in Shoshone Flats."

"Swindling? Swindling Abe? Why, you young whippersnapper. . . ."

Now, the man had insulted an officer. Ian was a whip snapper, not a whippersnapper.

Whomp! Ian's quirt handle slammed into the giant's stomach, a little below the belt because of the disparity in their sizes, and the big man doubled over in pain, bringing his head down so Ian did not have to jump to hit it. Whack! The quirt handle landed above the man's left ear. Ian considered it merciful to knock him unconscious since the first blow had been even lower than Ian intended.

"Look, Abe"—Ian turned to a pale Bernbaum—"I want this case off the docket fast, and I want the prisoner on my road gang. You can measure him for his jailhouse denims while he's laying here. Then I'll drag him over to the jail, though I might need Midnight's help. You bring a complaint for defrauding a merchant, and I'll get him for insulting a peace officer. You award yourself the twelve fifty for the suit, then give him three days or thirty dollars. I want his time, not his money."

Strangely befuddled, the usually reliable tailor bridled.

"Ian, this man is Jebediah Clayton. He's a Mormon, and you know how the mayor is about handling Mormons in town. This one even the Gentiles call J. C. in Shoshone Flat, so you can tell by his initials what the people think about him around here. He wasn't going to defraud me, not for one minute. He just likes to bargain. Besides, there's a legal question here. How can I be judge and plaintiff at the same time?"

Ian considered the situation for a moment. He was a reasonable man and did not want Mayor Winchester to consider him a pigheaded subordinate, too stiff-necked to abide by the town's policies. Personally, he did not wish to antagonize the Mormons since they were already using the road to trickle a few deposits into the bank, but the road had to go through. Also he was getting a reputation for being a fair man, evenhanded in his dispensation of punishment, and he did not wish to appear to be favoring the Mormons and the Hebrew by arresting only Gentiles.

"I declare, Abe, you're always confusing things. Trouble is, you don't know how to confuse them enough. Now, if you're bringing a false report against this man, just say so . . . I need an assistant water boy on my work gang . . . If you ain't, do as I say. Somebody's got to teach these Mormons to respect the law.

No, if you ain't bringing no false report, start measuring that man for his work clothes."

Abe reached into his pocket and began to unfold his tape measure.

"Ian, being the judge and plaintiff in this case doesn't strike me as being anywhere as irregular as being the judge and the defendant."

The input impinging on G-7's slightly diminished energy system was both encouraging and strangely disquieting.

Ian McCloud was becoming a living legend in the valley. It was as if the dwellers on this small segment of a planet—which, judged by one of its oldest records, the Bible, differed only in size and not in degree from Shoshone Flats—had been waiting for a strong man to appear. The citizens, incarcerated and free, were flocking around him. Disparate elements were being brought together to work for the common good, a good visible to all eyes. A shining high road of crushed rock and decomposed granite was stretching across the meadows. No one sought to question Ian's motives—those who knew his motives were tarnished were placated by their own gains—because the road was there and growing.

For the man himself, the idea of a road had become an obsession second only to Colonel Blicket. Principally because of the fines he had levied and the graft he was taking from his various enterprises, very few Gentile funds other than Ian's own and those of his cohorts were going into the bank. On the other hand, emboldened perhaps by the number of Gentiles in jail, the Mormons were beginning to use the bank more and more, and a new spirit of economic accommodation was making itself felt between the religious factions in the valley. Peace seemed imminent in Shoshone Flats.

Now, in an act completely contrary to his own interests, McCloud had arrested a Mormon. For nothing more than a keystone on the arch of a stone bridge, he had risked the fragile tranquillity of the community and his yet to be ill-gotten gains from the bank. He had arrested an honest, gentle, and lawabiding giant whom even Gentiles referred to reverently by his initials, J. C.

G-7 threw up its tendrils in despair. McCloud would have to work his way out of this dilemma alone, without the assistance of his guardian angel.

9

THROUGH his ability to transmit his drive and pride to the road gang, Ian got more than a rock mover from Jebediah Clayton. On the second afternoon of the big farmer's incarceration, as the scraper scraped, diggers dug, and, up ahead, Jebediah, already a section foreman in charge of a two-man crew, wheelbarrowed boulders from the hummock to the bridge site, Ian was again visited by the Avenging Angels.

Until the dark saints hove into view, it had been a pleasant afternoon for Ian seated astride Midnight atop a rise. Fleecy clouds floated above. Below him the spread skirts of picnicking young ladies dotted the meadow as they watched the stone span rise over the creek. Faintly to his ears came the "Heave, heave, ho" of a crew muscling a gravel wagon forward. Below him to eastward was a promontory overlooking the valley where Liza had told him Gabriella wanted to build her school—two acres or so jutting out into the farmlands of the senior Peyton.

When he spotted the black-coated cortege winding up from the south, Ian feared trouble. Now there were eight instead of six of the Latter-Day Saints, two more than the bullets in his revolver, and he was not a two-gun man.

Six bullets for eight saints!

Feeling the closest emotion to fear he had known since Gettysburg, Ian watched as the horsemen rode up the hill. Even if his gunslinging proved as sharp as the day he winged Billy Peyton, Ian thought, there was no way he could fire and reload in time to get them all. Of course, he could turn and flee. Heretofore flight had been his standard response to the approach of armed men. Now, pride and his investment in the valley prevented him from running.

As the Mormons drew nearer, Ian raised his left hand in greeting, Indian fashion, and Stake Superintendent Peyton raised his right hand in return. Old Man Peyton, Ian decided, was either intending to be reasonable or he knew no more about gunfighting than his son.

"Hello, deputy."

"Hello, super. What's the word from heaven?"

"Namoo tells me you've got one of my boys in your work gang."

The voice behind the smile was neither harsh nor hostile, but it was also neither importune nor placating.

Two of the riders were swinging behind Peyton, keeping away from the group and going higher up the hill to outflank Ian and get a clear angle of fire. Probably they were hired guns from Salt Lake City, Ian thought, and swerved his horse to keep them in his line of vision. He would have to get the gunfighters first and hope that in the resulting confusion a couple of the amateurs would shoot one another. Such mix-ups had been known to happen, but it was a slender reed to prop his life on.

G-7 fully agreed with Ian's estimate of the danger. Alerted by the deliberate approach of Peyton, G-7 had already disengaged its tendrils, leaving only a trailing filament attached to its host's otic nerve to register conversations. Invisible in the noonday sun, the nebulosity floated above McCloud.

The man's fate was solely in his own hands, for Ian's bright angel had left him.

"Yeah," Ian admitted, unaware that he had been deserted, "Jebediah Clayton got a little out of line yesterday, three days or thirty dollars' worth, by defrauding a Hebrew.''

"His arrest and sentencing was all legallike, I reckon."

Peyton's remark came perilously close to being a question, and Ian reacted quickly. "You ain't questioning the court's decision, are you, mister?"

Ian's words were a knife thrust Peyton parried with moderation. "Can't say I am, deputy."

"Good! Contempt of court could get you twenty days. . . . Except I might have trouble with the pussyfooting judge. He's been trying to get a little soft lately, and he might let you off with less. Maybe I ought to jail the judge for contempt of court. . . . But you ain't here to listen to my problems."

"Maybe the judge is the problem for both of us, deputy. The Hebrew's been giving you Gentiles thirty days or thirty dollars which figures out at one dollar a day. Then he ups and give J. C. three days or 30 dollars, which figures out at ten dollars a day. If the Hebrew had give J. C. three days or three dollars, the stake could have raised the fine. But, no. That son of Israel ain't being just with us Mormons."

On the record, the Mormons couldn't be trusted, Ian decided. They had brought eight men against a six-shooter, two of the men had tried to outflank him as they parleyed, and now the Mormon was trying to drive a wedge between the Hebrew and the Christian Gentiles to get the Christians over on the Mormon's side against the Hebrew.

"I ordered the ten dollars a day fine," Ian told him bluntly.

"Ain't that kind of high, deputy?"

Not only was the Mormon untrustworthy—he was unreasonable.

"High?" Ian flared. "It's low. Jeb's worth twelve ordinary Gentiles when it comes to hard work. Next to that red-haired Irishman, down yonder, J.C. is the best man I got. He'd be better than the Irishman, except Mickey O'Shea's got brains, and Jeb ain't."

Peyton eyed the deputy sheriff with confused understanding, as if giving Ian a new appraisal, and when he spoke, some of the iron was gone from his voice.

"You sound like a just man, deputy. . . . I know Jeb's a good worker. He's a law-abiding, God-fearing man, and he ought not to be in a jailhouse gang. He's got three wives and sixteen children to support."

"J. C. oughta thought about them before he set out to break the law," Ian snapped.

"But he ain't no lawbreaker, deputy."

Ian waved his hand toward the work gang below.

"Super, you go down and talk to any of them convicts. You won't find a one that ain't the most innocent, law-abiding, God-fearing man you ever met—by his own lights."

"I don't reckon no man's going to poor-mouth his self," Peyton admitted, "but I'm speaking up for J. C. He tithes regular."

"What's tithing?"

"He gives ten percent of all he makes to the church, like all good Mormons do."

Ian had not realized the Mormons were so generous, but with the knowledge he saw an opportunity.

"You think I ought to give J. C. ten percent off for good behavior," Ian asked harshly, "when the judge's done give him three days?"

Aware of the penalty for contempt of court, Peyton skirted the subject cautiously. "No, I ain't saying that. But J. C. is a head of families. Now, I brought you two unmarried boys, one's a tobacco chewer and the other smokes behind the barn, and I'll let you have them both for Clayton in a dead-even swap because these boys need discipline."

Peyton's remark explained the presence of the two scruffy-looking specimens farther up the hill; they were not flanking gunmen, they were outcast Mormons.

"Super, I ain't running no reform school for Latter-Day Saints, but seeing as how you and me always seem to hit it off, I'm willing to do you a favor. . . . You see that little point of land, down yonder, jutting off from the road?"

123

Still wary, Ian lifted his left hand and pointed down the hill beyond the road to the spur where O'Shea had piled the boulders from the blasting operation. Peyton followed the point with his gaze and nodded.

"That's your land," Ian continued. "If you're willing to donate it for a school for Miss Gabriella Stewart, I'd be willing to accept your proposal, but it would have to be between you and me, win, lose, or draw."

"Why between you and me?"

"I can't speak for Jebediah Clayton," Ian explained. "Jeb's sort of took a personal interest in the road, and he might not want to quit. For one thing, he's taking part in the dedication of the stone bridge tomorrow. He's placing the keystone in the arch by hisself. Another thing, he's got a suit of work clothes free that's all his own since no other prisoner in the territory's big enough to wear them, and Jeb, being honest, might figure he ain't earned them yet. Then J. C. might not be willing to go back to all them wives and children since he's got a taste of the free life in jail."

Peyton seemed to have forgotten Jebediah Clayton as he looked down on the point of land below. "There's nigh onto three acres of good farmland down there."

"Two acres of rock," Ian snorted.

"You put a Gentile school too near us folks, and our young ones will be wanting to go to it."

"Makes no difference. Book learning's book learning."

"I don't want to mix our angels with them Gentile angels," Peyton demurred. "Seeing as you got a powerful fondness for angels, deputy, you can understand that. I done lost one Mormon to the Methodists. He warn't much good, but I'd hate to lose a whole passel of good, tithing Mormons. . . . No, I couldn't give up them three acres for less than ten dollars an acre."

"Super, you can see from here that land's too rocky for farming. Them two acres ain't worth ten dollars an acre."

124

"I could lose ten tithing Mormons to that school," Peyton insisted.

"All Miss Stewart's going to teach is reading, writing, and ciphering," Ian said. "It's against the law to teach religion in school."

"If you're talking about the United States Constitution—" Peyton shook his head—"I don't know if it applies out here. Wyoming's a territory."

"I ain't talking about anybody's constitution. I'm talking about me. I'm the law in Shoshone Flats, and I'm saying there ain't going to be no talk about angels in that school, only the three R's. I ain't got nothing against Moroni or Namoo either, but I'm asking you this: Do you want to keep that miserable acre and a half of rocks, or do you want me to go down there and tell Jeb Clayton he's free to walk off his job, take them two boys of yours and break their tobacco habit, and put up a stone schoolhouse overlooking the valley like a monument—the Bryce Peyton Territorial School?"

A glow lighted Peyton's eyes and a sudden, warm enthusiasm came into his voice. "Deputy, ever since you started talking, that miserable half-acre of rocks is been getting smaller and rockier. If you'll let J. C. make his own choice and take them two jackleg saints up the hill there, the school land is yours."

Ian looked up the hill, regretting his own enthusiasm. The pair looked too seedy to really qualify for the road gang, and he could see no way to break the smoker's habit. Curing the tobacco chewer would be easy; he could break the man's jaw.

"Look, super. I'm running short of cell space. If J. C. ain't willing to make the trade for them two, does our bargain still hold?"

"All I want is my rights as stake superintendent," Peyton said. "If J. C. don't want his, that's up to J. C. Far as I'm concerned, the Bryce Peyton Territorial School is yours."

G-7 slunk back into its host, feeling pride mixed with chagrin. Ian had not needed its guidance, was, indeed, on the verge of scoring a coup for the community's good unassisted. The irony for G-7 was its awareness that McCloud must have had this scheme subconsciously in his mind when he ordered O'Shea to pile the rocks on the acreage.

What McCloud lacked in wisdom he made up in shrewdness and cunning, G-7 had to admit.

As Ian rode down the slope in the company of the stake superintendent, he realized he was taking a small but calculateed risk that Clayton might decide to go with Peyton, but Ian doubted it. The big man had been allotted a two-box ration of Liza's best chicken, and he had fallen in with the spirit of the road gang. As O'Shea had done, Clayton had developed an interest in stonemasonry and was personally involved in the construction of the bridge which had brought the largest turnout of female spectators in the history of territorial road building.

"Clayton, front and center," Ian yelled as they rode up.

The giant heaved a boulder he was carrying in the direction of the creek and loped over to the horsemen.

"Jebediah," Ian said, "Mr. Peyton's willing to swap two of his boys to serve out your time. He figures you're worth more to your family than you're worth to the people of Wyoming, or at least you're worth as much as a couple of his boys."

Clayton looked at Ian with disbelief and turned to glance at Peyton with scorn. When he spoke, he spoke only to McCloud.

"Deputy, if I ain't worth more than that, I ain't worth nothing. Anyhow, the mason's cutting the center stone tomorrow, and I'm the only man who can hoist it into place. I'm staying to see that bridge finished if the creek floods tomorrow and I have to wait a week."

Clayton turned and galloped back to the rock pile.

Shrugging his shoulders, Ian turned to the stake superintendent. "Trouble with these boys, Mr. Peyton, is that they're appreciated for what they're doing, and they appreciate what the others are doing. They don't get that kind of appreciation at home. You see I tried, but J. C. is bound and determined to finish that bridge, because I promised him the honor of putting the keystone in place."

"Well, he ain't bushwhacking our proposition," Peyton said. "You go ahead and put up that Bryce Peyton Territorial School, and I'll speak to the Elders about sending the children. You can have my eighteen young ones, that's a promise."

Riding back at the head of the column with O'Shea after quitting time, Ian said casually, "You seem sort of taken with stonework, Mickey. How'd you like to build a schoolhouse?"

"One thing at a time, boss. We haven't finished the road yet."

"I mean, how'd you like to be a contractor, build it for the town?"

"No, captain. This road's my last charitable contribution to Shoshone Flats."

"I ain't talking about charity, O'Shea."

"Begging your pardon, deputy, but if you're talking about building a schoolhouse for this town, you're talking about charity."

"You leave the contract up to me. How much do you figure it would cost the town for you to build a four-room schoolhouse out of native stone?"

O'Shea thought a moment before answering, "Not more than five hundred dollars."

"That's about what I figured," Ian agreed. "But I'll get you a contract for seven hundred, with a two-hundred-dollar advance for incidentals. You can pay me fifty for my half of the two hundred and you can pocket the rest. Is that fair?"

"You got a quick head for figures, captain," O'Shea said, "But I'm all for it."

After supper, Ian broached the subject to Mayor Winchester, who agreed to the proposal with reservations.

"O'Shea can't build a schoolhouse for any seven hundred dollars. I'll advance him the retainer, all right, from the administration fund, but I'd like to look over his cost figures. No sense letting that boy lose his shirt on his first contract with the town.

"Tell you what. You bring him by the church, Sunday. I'll go over the figures with him after the sermon, and I'll personally see to it that he gets back to jail."

O'Shea had not complimented Ian on his quick head for figures without a reason. After a few seconds' reflection, Ian realized that the mayor wanted to get the contractor alone only to raise the price of the schoolhouse, and Ian took immediate countermeasures to insure himself his share of the mayor's profits.

"Your word's as good as gold, Winchester, but I can't release a prisoner without a ten-dollar bond. That's a town ordinance."

"Of course," the mayor agreed, reaching for his wallet. "As mayor of this town, I'm always happy to abide by its ordinances, even the ones I forgot to sign."

Surprisingly for Ian, the only obstruction he encountered in his plan to construct the schoolhouse for Gabriella came from the prime contractor, Mickey O'Shea.

In a casual, offhand manner designed to cloak his intentions, Ian asked Gabriella if she had any pictures of buildings she liked. On Saturday evening after supper she dropped by the jailhouse office bringing a huge book, *Architectural Treasures of Europe,* which she laid on the sheriff's desk and opened to a full-page, mezzotinted engraving.

"Ian, I'd like to show you the world's most beautiful building, and I'd like to explain the architectural details which lead me to think so."

Rather dismayed by her tutorial manner, he demurred, "No use showing me Gabe, Mickey O'Shea's the man I want to look it over."

Turning, he shouted down the corridor, "O'Shea, front and center!"

O'Shea swung open his cell door and advanced at a quick step down the corridor, a questioning look on his face as he emerged into the office and noticed Gabriella.

Feeling that now was as good a time as any to make his intentions known to the girl, Ian waved his hand toward the book on the desk and said, "Mickey, take a gander at the schoolhouse you're building for Miss Stewart on Peyton's Point."

Across the desk from Ian, Gabriella's head snapped up, and she was looking at Ian in astonishment. A veil seemed to float over her eyes, and she continued to stare at Ian as O'Shea glanced at the picture.

Though Gabriella was petrified with amazement, her astonishment was less than O'Shea's. Leaning over the book, he, too, went rigid as a low whistle broke from his lips. Standing beside them, Ian waited patiently for the tableau to break, and O'Shea broke it first.

His voice rose to a high whine of incredulity as he said, "What the hell, boss? This is Chartres Cathedral."

"Watch your language, boy," Ian snapped, "There's a lady present. . . . Now, I don't care who owns the building, just shut up and build it."

Ian knew O'Shea would disobey the order because O'Shea had never heard it. In a stupefied monotone, he said, "It took four thousand Frenchmen four hundred years to build this building."

"Snap out of it, O'Shea. . . . Are you telling me you're willing to let a few Frenchmen outdo an Irishman?"

Gabriella was still in a trance caused by Ian's oblique announcement. O'Shea had turned pale, but he was continuing to argue.

"But, captain, Miss Stewart doesn't need a four-hundred-foot bell tower."

"Mickey," Ian explained patiently, gently, "she's got to have a building to impress them Mormons. Superintendent Peyton will be sending her his young ones, but that don't mean the others will fall in line. . . ."

"Ian McCloud, are you telling me that Bryce Peyton's already agreed. . . ." Finally, snapping out of her trance, Gabriella hurled the partial question, but O'Shea did not let her finish.

"Four hundred feet, captain. Don't you think that's overdoing it a mite?"

"Ian, I had no idea. . . ."

"Lop off a few hundred feet if you don't feel up to it," Ian said. "Maybe three hundred will be enough."

"Thirty's enough," Gabriella broke in. "But I don't need a bell tower. I have a hand bell. . . . Ian, what's this about Bryce Peyton?"

"Peyton's sending you his young ones."

"Let's see . . . eighteen young ones, that's thirty-six dollars, head tax," she said, and began to drift back into a trance when Ian aroused her.

"You'll need a bell tower, Gabe. No sense going out to ring your own bell on a rainy day, and a bell rope will have all the Mormon boys coming just to ring your bell. Anyhow, when that bell sounds, I want the whole valley to know there's a school in session."

"Then, by all means, give me a bell tower, Mr. O'Shea, but thirty-six feet will do fine."

"Make that a hundred, Mickey," Ian ordered.

"Oh, but Ian. . . ."

"No bother, Miss Stewart," O'Shea turned to the girl abruptly. "I believe I can satisfy both parties in regard to the height—one hundred feet for the captain and thirty for you."

"If you can do that, I'll be flabbergasted, but I'm already flabbergasted. For me, the most beautiful schoolhouse in the world, and right here in Shoshone Flats."

Standing, she seemed to be floating away, but O'Shea hardly noticed.

"What about the flying buttresses, Miss Stewart?" he asked, pointing to the page.

Gabriella had not heard O'Shea. She was drifting into a private world, her eyes misting over with happiness.

Ian glanced at the drawing on the page, to the abutments on the building O'Shea was pointing to, and he liked the looks of the exterior arches. They gave the building the straddlelegged stance of a gunfighter.

"I like them, Mickey, so throw in a few for her. Now, take the book and get cracking on them plans."

Strangely, O'Shea, also, seemed to be withdrawing. Standing over *Architectural Treasures of Europe,* staring down at the drawing, he was talking to himself. "A little Chartres. I never thought I'd start with a little Chartres."

Suddenly, he snapped out of his reverie, "Captain, I'll not only need the book, I'll need a drawing board, T squares, French curves, pencils, drafting paper, and five more days on my sentence."

"You ain't getting no more time from me, unless that road ain't finished on schedule. You're doing this on your own time."

Nevertheless, Ian had obtained the supplies from the general store by Monday, clearing almost as much from the purchase of the supplies as the $50 he earned from O'Shea's retainer fee. In addition, he permitted O'Shea to set up his drawing board in the cell-block corridor for night work and scheduled a day off from road work for a small crew under O'Shea to dig the foundations for the Peyton School. Ian's about-face followed the policy of generosity set by the town's administration. There was little point in being stingy with the prisoners' time since the mayor was not the saving sort. After reviewing O'Shea's plans for the school, Winchester had upped the contractor's bid to $910.27.

The mayor took the trouble to explain to the deputy why the contract had been upped; flying buttresses added considerably to a building's overhead. Ian admired the mayor's persuasiveness. He was convinced the additional cost was allowable until the banker greeted them on the sidewalk with a friendly, "Good morning, Mayor Winchester, Deputy McCloud."

Ian admired even more the twenty-seven cents Winchester tacked onto the bid. Such little touches separated mayors from deputy sheriffs.

Mormons were beginning to use the road now. Not only were the Mormons and Gentiles in the valley being drawn closer, Winchester and Bain, erstwhile symbols of virtue and vice in Shoshone Flats, were being seen together more often. Bain pledged $100 to the mayor's campaign fund to fight any possible reform candidate who might be entered into the race by the nonvoting wives of habitual poker losers.

Ian personally gained a feeling of accomplishment from the road. He was being paid well for his work, and the bank was gaining an increasing stream of depositors, but his feelings did not seem connected with the harvest, present and potential, he would gain in money. It was more a satisfaction in civic accomplishment, a pleasure alien to any he had ever felt before.

Full extent of the Winchester-Bain rapprochement was not brought home to Ian until the day of the ribbon-cutting ceremonies marking the opening of the road. Had it not been for the ceremonials planned by the mayor, Ian could have finished two days ahead of schedule and given the prisoners five days off for good behavior.

But the prisoners were not the only ones to suffer from the delay. Ian had to cancel his plans for a dramatic farewell to Gabriella since the ribbon cutting was posted for the afternoon he would have to leave to pick up the stagecoach at Wind River. Neither he nor she could avoid the ribbon cutting. The mayor had invited Ian to sit on the platform as a guest of honor, and Gabriella was to be the official ribbon cutter.

As it happened, Ian reached the official end of the road before eleven on the morning of September 2. A sizable crowd had gathered to watch the unofficial finish as the men worked toward the officials' platform and the wide swash of whitewash drawn across the road where the ribbon was to be strung. Ian's crew insisted on an impromptu ceremony of its own, handing him the last full shovel of gravel to spread on the last inch of road. Enough members of the band were on hand to tootle "For He's a Jolly Good Fellow" and give a festive note to the informal finish.

There was a spate of applause and handshakes for Ian after he bowed to the crowd and handed the shovel to O'Shea, who marched the crew smartly off to the jailhouse to wash up for dinner and get ready for the official ceremony at two o'clock. Both Gabriella and Liza were present, and they rushed up to buss his cheeks. He blushed and walked down the street, Midnight following.

Gabriella and Liza had to hurry back to the restaurant to prepare dinner for the prisoners and the expected large crowd. As Ian walked along, inwardly pleased but outwardly nonchalant, Billy Peyton fell into step beside him.

"Deputy, Miss Stewart mentioned you were interested in the fifty acres of my property between the Jebediah Clayton Bridge and the Bryce Peyton Territorial School."

"Yep."

"You can have the whole shebang for fifty dollars, provided you give me your word of honor you won't pay court to Miss Stewart."

The Methodists must have done a good job of converting on Peyton, Ian observed to himself, if the ex-Mormon was willing to trust a bank robber's word of honor, but here was a chance to make a fast $400 profit on land Sheriff Faust was willing to pay $500 for.

"Well, boy," Ian said, "I know I ain't up to courting Miss Stewart. She's got too much book learning to look on me as a legible suitor, but since you think different, let's step in the bank here and transfer the title. I got fifty dollars to spare."

Ian was pleased by the transaction and more pleased when Peyton immediately put the payment back into the bank. However, Ian's pleasure was short-lived. When he reached the office, he found Faust there attending to his administrative work by staying sober until after the ribbon cutting.

"Sheriff," Ian said, "I think I can get Billy Peyton's land for you for about five hundred, so's you can make your own beer when you retire."

Sober, Faust was suspicious. "Trying to retire me off, son? Getting ready to step into my boots while I'm still in them?"

"Naw, sheriff. Been thinking of quitting, myself. But you said you wanted the property."

"I did once, but that was before I brought law and order to Shoshone Flats. Doing administrative work sharpens a man, deputy. I decided to put my money in the bank and draw interest. By the time I retire, which ain't going to be for a long time yet, the people over in Idaho will be shamed into building a road to the Wyoming border to match the one Mayor Winchester ordered you to build. When that happens, the freight rates between here and the brewery in Pocatello's coming way down, and the price of beer's going to drop. With my interest money and the low prices, I figure I can buy more beer than I can brew in what little time I'll have left to me after I finally decide to retire."

Well, Ian thought, as he went to wash his hands, it served him right. He was a bank robber, not a hornswoggler, and it never paid to mix trades. But he'd lost nothing. He'd get his fifty dollars back, plus the sheriff's savings, tomorrow.

Ian's place of honor on the speaker's stand was to the left of the justice of the peace, who was left of the commissary stewardess who was left of the high sheriff, who was left of the ribbon cutter, who was left of the mayor. Strangely, Mr. Bain had been invited to the platform and sat to the right of the mayor. Prettily gowned and bonneted, Gabriella Stewart carried a large pair of shears at the ready. Before the platform, precisely ranked, shovels at "right shoulder," an honor guard of Ian's road crew under the command of Mickey O'Shea stood at attention.

After the crowd had assembled before the dignitaries and after a few patriotic airs from the band across the street, the mayor arose to "Present, tools!"—barked out by O'Shea. When O'Shea had ordered the honor guard to "Parade, rest!," the mayor introduced the honored guests from left to right, ending with Ian, "whose spadework under the supervision of Sheriff Faust made our dreams a reality."

When Ian arose to acknowledge the introduction, prolonged applause and cries of "Speech, speech" arose from the crowd, so the mayor invited Ian to say a few short words.

"When I first got here," Ian said, "I had two complaints about this town—the Mormon gunfighter couldn't shoot straight and Dead Man's Curve was too crooked. Since then, your Mormon gunfighter's become a Methodist straightshooter and O'Shea's Gap has straightened out Dead Man's Curve. Now, I ain't got no complaints.

"However, I'm giving all my convicts time off for good behavior, right after ribbon cutting, and inviting them over to Bain's Saloon to have free drinks on me. If any of the rest of you have been saving up for a spree, tonight's the night to throw it. I'm leaving here for Wind River to ride shotgun on the stage, right after the ribbon cutting, and I won't be back till tomorrow morning. So, tonight, I won't be arresting nobody. Thank you."

Amid prolonged cheers, Ian sat down, and the mayor arose to wait out the silence. When it finally came, Mayor Winchester went into a spiel describing the future of Shoshone Flats, which Ian had heard before in Brother Winchester's description of heaven, then with the added attraction of a radiant throne.

Ian's thoughts wandered to his own immediate future.

Blicket would hit the stagecoach at sunrise, the way he always did. Probably he'd detail The Sergeant to kill the rear guard and fluster the driver, then The Colonel would step around the corner of the cliff on the big gray and get the drop on the driver, lulling the man with honeyed words to make him feel safe and to watch the surprised look on his victim's face when he pulled the trigger on his sawed-off shotgun. Colonel Jasper Blicket was right fond of surprises.

But The Colonel and his orderly would make a mistake. They'd think it was Johnny Loco riding rear shotgun on the stagecoach, and there'd be no means of identification afterwards because The Sergeant used lead minié balls with a slit across the nose, dum-dum bullets named for the sounds they made going in and coming out. But the final remains of the shotgun guard would not be the scraps of Johnny Loco, for he would be crouched inside the stagecoach waiting.

Somehow, Ian's daydreams about the coming fracas weren't as pleasing as they should have been. After going six weeks without killing a man, his bloodthirst should have been sharp; he should have been snorting for the smell of gunpowder. Maybe he was getting out of the habit of killing people.

Maybe he could even break the habit if he wanted to, and that was the strangest thought of all.

Ian became alert to the final sentences of the mayor.

"Knowing our deputy will be fully taken up by his law-enforcement duties under the capable administration of our beloved old-timer, Sheriff Faust, I have contracted for the remainder of our town's roads to be graveled by private means. To supervise this great work, I have called upon a merchant well known and well served by us all. We will now hear a few words from Mr. Timothy J. Bain, our new Commissioner of Public Roads."

Ian knew he was being scrouged out of a place at the road fund trough, that Bain was being paid off, politically, for his support of the mayor, but it mattered little. After he had killed The Colonel and The Sergeant, he would circle back, wait for the bank to open, and make off with the road fund, administration fund and all the other funds. He would ride north on a horse that couldn't be caught through Gentile country, where every able-bodied man for miles around would be suffering from hangover and indifferent to any call to join a posse.

For once, a straightshooter was going to win out over a politician.

Bain arose to say that he appreciated the honor conferred

upon him by the town's beloved mayor and that he would continue the policy so ably begun under the mayor's administration by putting gravel on the remainder of the roads in the metropolitan area of Shoshone Flats. Since the contract to gravel the roads had already been let by the able and energetic mayor, his first official duty as road commissioner would be to dedicate the first finished portion of the road network.

At a nod from the mayor, Gabriella had descended from the platform to stand by the ribbon, and Bain continued, "So now, Miss Stewart, stand by as I take great pleasure in naming this road with a name that symbolizes our future and honors our past. You may cut the ribbon, Miss Stewart."

Gabriella cut. As the ribbon fluttered to the ground, Bain continued, "I hereby formally open the new Winchester Pike."

As Gabriella whirled, eyes flashing, hands on hips, a loud shriek arose from under a sunbonnet far back in the audience. "It's McCloud's road. Why don't you call it that—McCloud's Road?"

Amid derisive hoots and catcalls, the honor guard turned with drawn shovels and would have climbed the platform to belabor the new commissioner if O'Shea had not barked, "Stand fast, you scalawags! There's more to come."

Smiling benignly, raising his hand to silence the jeers of the crowd, Commissioner Bain bellowed above the tumult, "Ladies and gentlemen, Deputy McCloud has not been forgotten. Let our mayor speak."

"He'd better talk fast," Jebediah Clayton yelled, shouldering his vast bulk toward the platform, and the mayor responded, talking fast.

"Because of Deputy McCloud's great contribution to the actual construction of the road and because of its part in bringing Gentile and Mormon closer together in this valley, we have reserved a special honor for Deputy Ian McCloud."

Watching Jebediah Clayton advance, Winchester sacrificed eloquence of speech for a rapid delivery.

"Fifty yards south of here, on the spot, yonder, where you

see the boulders piled, your road commissioner has contracted with our general contractor, Mr. Michael O'Shea, to erect a stone building along the lines of the Taj Mahal, with the addition of architectural features our deputy is particularly fond of, which should prove a welcome addition to the ladies of the community.''

J. C. stopped and the mayor continued at a more eloquent pace.

"We Gentiles in the valley cherish our ladies because of their rarity, but we must welcome the wives of our Mormon friends and look also to their comfort. Today, we have no facilities at all for the fair sex. The barbershop is a male tonsorium. The hotel is infested with drummers. Ladies do not enter the barroom. So, even before Mr. O'Shea commences construction of the Bryce Peyton Territorial School, he is going to hasten the immediate construction of the Ian McCloud Comfort Station which will be large enough to accommodate six ladies simultaneously.''

Applause swelled from the throng as the mayor sat.

Fearing now that no force this side of heaven could divert McCloud from his self-appointed ends, G-7 felt itself comforted by the mayor's announcement. Through an instrumentality it had considered even less likely than McCloud, peace and religious unity might be coming to the valley, and G-7 was grateful. Although for the time being it was no longer fighting to save mankind—only the one man—it welcomed all the help it could get in the fulfillment of its larger aims, and the mayor's gesture was providential.

Not even the sight of its spaceship, lying slightly apart from the other building stones beside the road and apparently scheduled to be the cornerstone for the privy, disturbed G-7's appreciation for the turn of events. It was not alone in its striving for the common good. While it watched its chosen host careen toward a confrontation with evil, its work toward religious brotherhood had found an ally in a low, grafting politician, the mayor.

G-7 was still blessing Winchester when a strangely furious

Liza leaned across the justice of the peace and whispered to McCloud, "There's a lot of talk about giving the women the vote in Wyoming. That old four-flusher's stacking his deck with your cards. In this valley, the Mormons' vote is the women's vote, what with all their wives. Winchester's aiming to corral the Mormon vote. He don't care nothing for the ladies' comfort. He's using your good name to get hisself reelected."

Bernbaum nodded and intoned a solemn, "Selah!"

Though he knew the widow spoke the truth, Ian was not disturbed. In fact, he was well pleased. To his knowledge, there was not another outlaw in the whole West who had a six-holer named in his honor.

10

FROM Wind River to Shoshone Flats, the stage route wound over mountains. Night turned chilly in the high altitudes, which gave Ian an excuse for riding inside the stagecoach, but, in addition to his plan to ambush the robbers, he had another reason for wanting to ride inside—squeamishness. He did not wish to get too friendly with either the driver or the rear guard, knowing they would both be dead by sunrise.

Ian could not understand his concern for his horse. Tied to the rear of the stagecoach, plodding along at a fraction of his normal pace, Midnight might grow chill from the lack of exercise. His sensitivity toward the men bothered Ian.

After pulling this job, he decided, he might invest some of his loot in railroad stocks, learn something about railroading, and take to robbing trains. A man had to progress with his times, and the future was in railroads. He was getting too picayunish and too smart for outdoor work.

Although he tried to doze, he was constantly being awakened as the stage lurched and pitched on the upgrade. Past midnight, after he heard the clunk of brake shoes on the iron rims of the wheels, all desire for sleep left him. The stagecoach had topped the crest and was heading down. By dawn, it should reach the stretch of road where the mountains dropped sharply to a canyon's floor. At that point, with the cliff almost sheer to the left and a five-hundred-foot drop to the right, the road took a sharp bend around the cliff and became too narrow for the driver to take evasive action. Here, Ian figured, The Colonel would place a barricade and wait around the bend. Probably The Sergeant would hide among the boulders above the road and gun down the guard from the rear, figuring he was killing Johnny Loco.

Tension was growing in Ian's mind, and, unknown to McCloud, it was a dual tension. The being inside was growing more alert.

Outside the window, the first faint glow of sunrise was touching the canyon's rim to eastward. Ian removed from his lap the shotgun furnished by the stage line and unholstered his revolver, sliding to the floor of the coach to conceal his silhouette from a watcher outside. He was crouched low, his legs spread, his left hand on the door handle and his right on his pistol.

A shotgun was impractical for Ian's purposes. At the close range he figured The Colonel would be, a blast from a shot gun would tear his victim in two, and he wanted The Colonel to die slowly. It didn't matter about The Sergeant. He would die like the animal he was, specifically an ape, but The Colonel was a man of sensibilities, a Southern gentleman.

A Southern gentleman!

G-7 sensed a residual respect in the term its host verbalized, a remnant aura of an old regard, and it seized on the connotations.

It responded to the tensions in the mind of McCloud with its own tensions, resolving that this man must be saved. It would never again desert its host. It settled its tendrils firmly along the neuron channels of the man's brain and tapped the brain's obsession, using the feedback to power a counterobsession, stroking McCloud's beta waves.

Hatred had carried McCloud down this tortuous trail to his showdown with Blicket, and McCloud had never faltered from his purpose. Would the love which had arced the galaxies endure less? The heavens forbid! G-7 nursed the one area of near-warmth in the ice-mind of McCloud, charged it, enhanced it with coiling tendrils of light.

A Southern gentleman.

Unaccountably, Ian relaxed slightly on the floor of the coach, thinking; he'd learned a few things from Blicket, he had to admit. When he first met The Colonel and was admitted to his outlaw band on the strength of a service record as a Confederate sharpshooter—seventeen Yankees killed, seven wounded— The Colonel had been solicitous of Ian's well-being. The older man had gone out of his way to impress on Ian the value of planning in a successful holdup, and The Colonel was one of the softest-talking men Ian had ever met.

It had been a pleasure just to listen to The Colonel use the language; that and his military flair had a way of making every job sound interesting. Their last holdup of a U.S. Cavalry squadron had been like old times during the war, with Ian decoying the bluecoats up a draw into ambush while Blicket directed operations from behind the lines.

He had never tried to understand the man, Ian admitted, but only obeyed orders. Squatting now on the floor of the lurching stagecoach, Ian ransacked his memories of Colonel Blicket, trying to understand the man's behavior and groping, subconsciously, toward the principle that to understand all was to forgive all.

Blicket's life had forced the man to become a harsh disciplinarian. As a brevet colonel commanding a squadron of irregulars in Quantrill's guerrillas, Blicket's troops had been mostly barn burners, night riders, bushwhackers, and border ruffians—the scummiest bunch of murderers on horseback ever assembled—and the mildest form of discipline such men understood was a pistol-whipping.

Then, after the war, Blicket was at loose ends. He could not retain his commission in the army because he had fought on the wrong side; in fact, he was second after Wirtz on the Federals' wanted list. Since he was too skinny to be a plowboy and not crooked enough to be a lawyer, the end of the war had left The Colonel only the skills of shooting, riding, and commanding men. Society was responsible for Colonel Blicket because society had let peace be declared.

Ian could see the tangled web of the man's life with startling clarity and even more startling sympathy. If he could sit down and have a heart-to-heart talk with The Colonel, he might point out the folly of the man's ways. He would have only one problem in talking to Blicket—they would have to yell at each other across a space of twenty yards, the lethal range of The Colonel's sawed-off shotgun.

Now half-slumped in his reveries, Ian suddenly tensed, realizing the incongruity and danger in his sympathy. Talking to Blicket would be as sensible as patting a rattlesnake's head, for once the Colonel started to sweet-talk a man, that man was as good as dead. He had to rid himself of such thoughts immediately, purge his mind of deadly compassion.

Ian had the purgative at hand. Quite deliberately, he took a deep breath, exhaled slowly, and summoned into his mind the conscious memory of an insult.

Knowing now that Ian's motive and his cure for passion was about to be revealed, G-7 wrapped its tendrils tighter around the neuron paths in the man's brain and waited.

In memory, Ian stood again, invisible in the shadows of the ravine, hearing the voices of The Colonel and The Sergeant drift up the draw after Garcia had been killed.

First he heard the rumble of The Sergeant's voice.

"Loco might think his horse throwed that shoe accidental and try walking to the rendezvous. Reckon I ought to backtrack and kill him, too?"

"No, Sergeant" came the soft, well-modulated tones of The Colonel. "Loco's not worth the effort. Kill Garcia's horse to deny him a beast to ride and leave him to the mercy of the desert. A slow death will give him time to consider his errant ways, for the man lied to me in a most reprehensible manner."

Then The Colonel's voice dropped letting an eternal note of sadness in.

"Yes, Sergeant, the man you knew as Johnny Loco was Ian McCloud, an ambulance driver in the Army of McClellan. The poltroon who posed to us a rebel sharp-shooter was, in truth, a blue-bellied Yankee."

Blue-bellied Yankee!

The insult triggered a cyclonic fury in the mind of the man, which swept G-7 into its vortex. G-7's tendrils quivered. Fully aware that it was losing its objectivity, becoming involved, G-7 was no longer an observer. It shared the anger of its host.

By what arrogance could a barn burning, woman killing, temporary colonel in charge of a ragtag outfit of jayhawkers presume to defame a four-year veteran of Lee's Miserables with such a term.

Blue-bellied Yankee, indeed.

But a dastard who planned every move had overlooked a simple fact; it was not a horse Ian needed to escape from the desert but a horseshoe. Moreover, Ian found a hammer in the revolver of the dead Garcia with which to drive the nails taken from Garcia's dead horse. It was fitting and somehow just that defective planning and Garcia's pistol should prove the fatal flaws of Colonel Jasper Blicket.

G-7 was eager for the kill.

Ian was eager, and ready, when the brake shoes clumped against the wheels with enough friction to bring the stagecoach to a jolting halt. Beginning with dactyls and soaring to strophes and antistrophes, a mule skinner's metric profanity sounded from the driver's seat, but the tirade against the luck of the road reached its climax in a blast of rifle fire from somewhere to the rear of the stagecoach. Ian heard the rear guard's body slam against the roof of the vehicle, and he knew the man was dead. The Sergeant, also, had been a sharpshooter with Quantrill's guerrillas.

From forward, he heard the Colonel's voice crying up to the driver, "Just hold where you are, sir. You will not be harmed, I assure you. My apologies for having to discommode you in so drastic a manner. All we desire is the payroll box at your feet. Be so kind as to throw it to The Sergeant, sir, and you'll be permitted to continue your journey in peace to give your fallen comrade a decent Christian burial, though, familiar as I happen to be with the dead gentleman in question, I allow that the blue belly was not much of a Christian."

It was The Colonel's method, Ian knew, to feed his victim honeyed words to make the killing easier, to enhance the element of fatal surprise, then throw in an insult to the dead. Once the driver had tossed the box down and completed all the heavy labor, he too would be killed with the sawed-off shotgun The Colonel preferred for close-in shooting.

Without looking out, without seeing the scene, Ian could spot the location of each actor from the sounds: The Colonel atop the gray was forward of the stagecoach horses, the Sergeant scuffling down from the rocks in which he had hidden for the ambush. Ian felt the stagecoach creak as the driver stood to heave the payroll box down, and he heard the man grunt as he released the weight.

Ian opened the door and leaped from the coach.

G-7 fissioned an ion.

Once more, time froze around Ian. He floated out of the stagecoach and drifted toward the ground. Fluttering like a leaf, he twisted in flight and fired a bullet toward the heart of The Sergeant who stood slightly up the hillside, his simian arms lifted to catch a box which was falling slower than the bullet which moved toward his heart. Ian spun farther in his gyre, clockwise relative to the ground, knowing The Sergeant would never catch the box alive. He heard a "splat" as his bullet struck The Sergeant's sternum before he heard the slowly ascending "kapow" of his pistol, which was merging into the long withdrawing roar of the shotgun's blast. With his right arm held high for balance, he landed lightly on the balls of his feet to face The

Colonel who, teeth bared in a grin was sending a charge of buckshot crawling upward toward the driver.

As Ian's boot heels came slowly level with the balls of his feet, he brought the pistol down from the height it had reached when he flung his arm. Beneath The Colonel's head, Ian's gaze caught the gray uniform of an officer of the Confederacy. He could not find within himself enough sacrilege to despoil the uniform, so he halted the downward progress of his pistol and took careful aim at The Colonel's head, denying himself a groin shot for the patriotic reason.

Colonel Blicket was turning to the sight and sound of Ian, and his head bent slowly in Ian's direction. Like a lover bending to savor a kiss, he accepted the caress of the bullet precisely between the eyes, and the "zap" the slug made against the bridge of his nose sounded, ironically, as sensuous as a kiss. As his head snapped slowly back, straining against a neck which dragged his long body off the horse, time resumed its tempo amid the roar of gunfire echoing and reechoing from the canyon walls.

In the interstices of frozen time, G-7 found space to reevaluate its loss of objectivity. It had, itself, indulged a certain pleasure in scrambling the energy systems of The Colonel and The Sergeant, both of which richly deserved cessation. For a moment during the gunfight, it had enjoyed a rare and total rapport with its host, but now that the fighting was over the slow process of reformation would have to be resumed.

By all its canons and creeds destructiveness was a sin. In a moment of passionate weakness it had yielded to the profligacy of the planet, and now it and its host must atone. Casting on Ian's visual areas the image of Gabriella, her face frozen into lines of disapproval, it triggered a phrase of self-revulsion in McCloud's mind.

"Look on this waste, you violent, and despair."

Ian glanced around him.

Nothing had been wasted here. Gabriella with her saving ways ought to appreciate this gunfight. Four bullets had been fired and four people were dead.

But, he was forced to admit, the carnage might have reinforced Gabriella's dislike of violence. The Colonel's shotgun blast had driven the driver backwards, and he was spread-eagled atop the stagecoach, gazing at the risen sun with his one good eye. The right side of his face had been torn away by the charge and the right eyeball, a viscous glob stringing from an attenuated eye muscle, dangled over his cheekbone and seemed to be studying intently something on the ground. To the rear, the shotgun guard's condition might have also upset Gabriella. The Sergeant's dum-dum bullet had entered the back of the man's head, carrying most of his face with it and scattering his brains and bits of skull as far as the driver.

On the ground, only The Sergeant looked natural, lying on his back against the hillside with his face unmarred. His sloping forehead, his heavy eyebrows almost touching his black, kinky hair, made him appear more apelike than human. The only unnatural aspect of The Sergeant was his eyes, open and staring at the sun. There was more expression in them, dead, than Ian had ever seen in them, alive.

It was a monstrous scene, Ian admitted, even to a person with only a clinical interest in the details, but not until he turned to the recumbent form of The Colonel did the taste of death turn to ashes in his mouth. Patting the rump of the giant gray with proprietary interest, he walked to the rear of the horse and looked down.

Ian's bullet had drilled a hole neatly between The Colonel's eyes, giving him a three-eyed face. Pressure from the bullet going in had bulged the eyes outward and turned them inward, so, in effect, The Colonel's normal death's-head appearance, accentuated by his baldness, retained the illusion of reality slightly distorted which gave the corpse a grotesquerie greater than the others. Ian was looking down on a cross-eyed, bug-eyed monster.

Yet it was not the horror that brought sadness to Ian: It was the knowledge that Colonel Blicket died before he knew who killed him. For any personal satisfaction it gave him, Ian might as well have shot a hole in a fence post, and for all Colonel Blicket *knew,* he could have died a pillar of the community, surrounded by eager heirs and a grieving widow. The clod stretched out before Ian was as incapable of hating or being hated as a fallen legionnaire of Julius Caesar.

Still, Ian doffed his hat out of respect for the uniform and stood for a moment with bowed head. "Vengeance is mine, saith the Lord" was a part of the Scripture he understood fully now. Only the Lord had the power, if the Lord had a mind to, to get to a man after he was dead and explain to him the error of his ways.

It behooved Ian to think good thoughts about the dead, and the nicest thing he could think about The Colonel was that he had left a good horse for Ian McCloud, not counting The Sergeant's nag which was built more for carrying weight than for speed. Looking over at The Sergeant, the best thought Ian could think about him was that, as brutal, moronic, and sadistic as The Sergeant had been, he was a more righteous man than The Colonel, mainly because he didn't have brains enough to make him worse.

Then, too, he was obliged to the two of them for killing the driver and guard.

Suddenly, Ian's mind soared above funereal thoughts. Horses weren't the only valuable items around here. Three thousand dollars in greenbacks were in the payroll box. He turned and clambered up the hill.

When the driver tossed the payroll cash down, the heavy wooden container had either hit The Sergeant's head as Ian turned away or it had hit a boulder and bounced up the hillside. When it fell, one of the planks had loosened. As Ian bent and pried back the loose board, he looked in and saw neat stacks of ten dollar bills banded in groups of ten and so fresh he could smell the ink. Thirty such bundles lay before him, all his.

G-7 had tensed for another confrontation with evil, but its direct-line reasoning had not prepared it for the storm which swept McCloud's brain when his eyes fell on the money. It was almost shaken from the neuron channels along which it lay, relaxing from its efforts in computing the trajectories of the gunfighter's bullets and slowing his concept of time. Writhing in the hail of neurons, G-7 recoiled from the storm center, the thalamus. Never before had it truly gauged the extent of this man's greed.

That greed must be counteracted at once, or the cosmic storm whipping through the hydrocarbons of its host would deetherealize G-7. The being was no longer fighting to save mankind or Ian McCloud. It was fighting for its own existence.

Frantically, G-7 fissioned an ion, nudging a carbon atom here, realigning a molecular chain there, quieting axions, plugging synapses, firing into the cerebral cortex impulses toward social duty, self-respect, obedience to law, human decency, honesty, goodness, unselfishness. It thought it was calming the storm until Ian reached in and picked up a stack of bills and riffled the edges. They were crisper to his touch than a new deck of cards, and the odor of their ink was more potent than the perfume of Gabriella.

Gabriella! Recoiling farther from the thalamus, G-7 sent photons against the visual areas of Ian's brain and projected a picture of Gabriella, poised, beautiful, but smiling down on him with disapproval.

What a time for wool-gathering about a single girl, Ian thought. With this $3,000 plus the money in the bank, he could have every beauty south of the border, then rent a private railroad car to take him to New England for a fling with Yankee girls, girls who would not be fencing him in with the "do's" and "don'ts" of a schoolteacher. He bent for another packet of tens to fondle.

G-7 fused two ions and fissioned them as one.

With its new burst of power, G-7 laid before its host a veritable feast of the pleasures of respectability and domesticity.

It revealed to the man's inner vision the delights of a cottage with a rose garden, the esteem of neighbors, loving babes, an adoring and faithful wife, Gabriella. As Ian fanned the bills like cards before him, G-7 wrought in his mind its own version of the Temptation on the Mount.

Ian was not tempted by the appeals of domesticity and respectability. G-7 might as well have appealed to his sense of honor and duty. Ian was shuffling the bills and sniffing them.

Borrowing from the habits of its host, G-7 dropped its straight-line reasoning and drew to an inside straight.

It curved into Ian's thalamus a three-dimensional image of Liza charged with G-7's own high regard for the earth mother. It was a portrait of the woman's head and her robust torso, heaving and bare. But a sadness in the widow's eyes denied to the man her torso's promise of pneumatic bliss.

G-7 filled to a royal flush.

"By golly," Ian said, lifting his head to sniff around him the faint and sulfurous reek of ionized hydrogen, "I never thought of that."

With her head for business, no wonder Liza disliked the way he was handling this matter. The Colonel over yonder was worth $5,000 dead, and The Sergeant was worth $3,000. Together they were worth almost twice as much as the $3,000 in the box, even though it would take two or three days to collect the rewards. The $7,000 he'd make from the bounties would make him such a heavy depositor to the Shoshone Flats bank he'd lose more in interest than he'd gain from robbing the bank.

Besides, Shoshone Flats was the closest town to the new Indian reservation, and he'd always had a feeling of sympathy for the Indians. They were the CSA of the West because they'd lost their war, too. Staying in town, he might be able to do something nice for the poor, cooped-up Indians.

He tithed four packets of tens for himself from the payroll money and nailed the loose plank back onto the box with his boot heel. The money would be missed, but the Territorial Stage

Lines was responsible for the bookkeeping. If the stage line lost its contract through the dishonesty of its bookkeepers, it would serve Birnie right for hiring just anybody who would work for the wages Birnie paid.

He hoisted the box back onto the driver's platform and lugged the body of The Sergeant over and tossed it lengthwise onto the floor of the coach. Showing deference to the uniform, he set The Colonel's body on the seat, tilting the head against the side of the stagecoach and dropping the wide-brimmed campaign hat over the three eyes. Too bad, Ian thought, that there was no sword to lay on The Colonel's chest.

He backed out of the stage quickly and walked forward to gather the horses. He didn't mind the odor of blood since it came with the job, but he didn't like the odor of ozone which hovered in the area as if lightning had struck nearby. His mother, he remembered, always said it smelled like brimstone.

After he rounded up the gray and The Sergeant's stocky pinto, the odor had drifted away, and Ian got a pleasant surprise. When he tied the gray back of the stage next to Midnight, the black horse whinnied softly and the gray nickered in reply. This solved a problem he was already beginning to worry about, one that might have interfered, even, with his new plans; it hadn't struck him before but The Colonel's gray, Traveler II, was a mare.

He lassoed the brake handle by the driver's seat and, trailing the lariate over his shoulder, mounted one of the lead horses. He could brake the stagecoach by tugging on the rope, and he did not want to sit on the driver's seat next to the late driver. Without a doubt, he was losing his stomach for this business, so the decision he had made was the right one.

For the second time in a month, almost to the day, Ian rode into Shoshone Flats astride a draft horse, trailing a grisly burden behind. For the second time, he was greeted first by the sunbonnet under which dwelled his most loyal support, Sister Betsy Troop, who stood by the stakes which marked the future site of the McCloud Comfort Station.

"Who you bringing in this time, Ian?"

"Colonel Jasper Blicket and one of his gang, a fellow called The Sergeant. I don't recall the names of the two gentlemen on top."

"The driver used to be Graves Paige," Sister Betsy said. "Lived over near Jackson City. Never took him for the brainy kind, but I can see he had his share. Poor boy, done give his all for the Territorial Stage Lines. Don't recognize the other one because he ain't got no face. . . . Well, as I always said, crime don't pay."

"This one will," Ian disagreed. "Them two inside's worth about $7,000; $3,000 for the enlisted man and $5,000 for the officer, respectfully."

"Crime might pay more if you'd learn how to add," Sister Betsy volunteered, "or if you'd pull down them window curtains and charge twenty-five cents a peek to this crowd coming here."

"Don't want people paying to see that crime don't pay," Ian said.

Attracted by the growing throng that trailed or walked abreast of the stagecoach, a few walking backwards in front of the stagecoach, Gabriella came out of the restaurant to wave gaily to Ian. He saluted her, but when she looked up at the driver, back at the guard, and peered in at the last soldiers of the Lost Cause, she turned and ran back into the restaurant. Her face was white and she was holding both hands over her mouth, and he knew she was running to the slop jar to throw up.

It occurred to him, then, that a woman should not be judged by her parts but in her totality. It was not enough that a female should have lean flanks—there was also the matter of a strong stomach. Gabriella's stomach, he was forced to admit, tended to be a mite weak.

On the other hand, Liza, emerging from the stage line's office after a chicken box delivery, looked on the scene with nothing but admiration.

"Looks like you run into a peck of trouble, Ian, but looks like you managed to handle it, as usual," she called up to him. "Who you got inside there? General Lee?"

"No'm. He was just a brevet colonel."

"If them things was alive, you'd have yourself the goldarndest sideshow, ever, of traveling freaks."

"Sister Betsy had partly the same idea," Ian told her as he slid from the horse. "If you're going to be in town for another half hour, I'd like to see you in the sheriff's office after I turn this coach over to the Jackson City crew and make arrangements to collect my bounty."

"That won't take no half hour."

"No'm, but I got to stop by the bank. . . . I'm impounding them saddle horses, Liza, as stolen goods. How'd you like to own the gray?"

Liza looked at the horse and whistled her appreciation. "Has a chicken got feathers? That's a five-hundred-dollar horse, Ian. You willing to give it to me?"

"If you're a reasonable woman."

"Boy, you're looking at the reasonablest woman the good Lord ever created."

Ian's affairs took longer than half an hour because he found a wrong that needed righting and, in the righting thereof, took his first unassisted step toward respectability and civil responsibility.

The stage line's relief crew was waiting to drive the coach on to Jackson City. Ian sent word by it to the federal marshal there that he had taken The Colonel and The Sergeant into custody, dead, and would hold the bodies for official identification. While Birnie made arrangements to send the bodies of the driver and guard back to Wind River, Ian conscripted four spectators to carry the dead outlaws to Near-Sighted Charlie's office. Ian bade the entourage to wait outside since Charlie's sod-covered icehouse was behind the undertaking establishment, and he entered.

Strangely, Near-Sighted Charlie balked at storing the bodies. "Who's paying the five dollars for the service, deputy? Ice costs money."

Charlie was lying, Ian knew; he chopped the ice out of the river each winter free of charge, but the question did pose an administrative problem. If Ian left the bodies on the sidewalk, crowds of curious onlookers would slow the traffic and put the problem under the jurisdiction of the road commissioner and the road fund. If the corpses were left in the sunlight for two or three days, the town would have to be evacuated and the evacuation would be the mayor's responsibility, an expense of the administration fund.

Ian decided to take first things first and told Charlie, "I'll sign a five-dollar draw on the road fund, and you collect from Bain."

"Won't do no good, deputy. Mayor Winchester passed an ordinance yesterday that no name's to be honored on the road fund but Commissioner Bain's."

If only an administrative problem had been involved, this information would have prompted Ian to leave the bodies on the sidewalk, but he had a financial interest in preserving the physical identity of the outlaws.

"What difference does it make whose signature it is? You can't see it nohow."

"I heard your voice, deputy, so I know you're out there, and the mayor said, in particular, that the deputy sheriff's signature was no longer to be honored."

Administrative hedges Ian could understand, but to be singled out for a loss of an honest privilege was another matter. A cold rage seized him. While he had been out of town for less than twenty-four hours, answering the call of civil duty, protecting the public, the mayor had been slipping around his back, fencing him out from the trough. Ian had known this was occurring, yesterday, but it had not mattered to the badman he had been yesterday. Now he was going straight, and the first time, ever, he reached into the till for a legitimate expense, the mayor slammed the drawer on his fingers.

The minute Ian finished the road, he had been spurned by the official who had used him. For the only time in his life, Ian was suffering an undeserved injustice, and the mayor's treachery rankled. In plain view of an ordinary man, he bent over Charlie's desk and wrote out a five-dollar chit, signing it.

"Here's your chit, Charlie. There's your bodies. This paper's as good as gold. You can take my word."

"What other collateral can you give me?"

"Winchester on a slab, and no cutback to me on his funeral expenses."

The iron ring in Ian's voice brought a smile of agreement to the undertaker's face. "Knowing you and knowing him, I figure I'm bound to get paid one way or the other."

Charlie turned and called outside, "Take the departed ones to the icehouse, boys."

Striding from the undertaker's to the bank, Ian managed to rein his anger with a brand-new halter—objective detachment. Killing Winchester would not teach the mayor the error of his ways. Besides, the mayor was also a preacher; murdering him might not set well with most of his congregation, would lower Ian's standing as a law-abiding citizen in the community, and any public official who figured out a way to tap the public till six days a week *and* Sunday deserved a more subtle chastisement than a bullet in the head.

Suddenly he had an idea. He could teach the mayor humility without having to pistol-whip the preacher, and the solution to the Winchester problem lay in Bain, the biggest contributor to the mayor's campaign fund.

Three minutes after he left the bank, Ian shouldered through the swinging doors of the saloon and moved along the bar toward the back room, ignoring Faust at his beer-drinking station. As he moved, Ian was conscious that he was passing a milestone in his life and taking a giant stride toward respectability. He was going to complete his first commercial arrangement kept entirely within the letter of the law.

Seated at his desk and totaling a column of figures, Bain

looked up and began a nervous smile of greeting to his visitor, which was quickly squelched by the hostility of McCloud.

"Bain, I liked the way you and Winchester tried to squeeze me out of the road fund."

"It wasn't my idea, deputy. The mayor didn't like the way you disobeyed his orders and run in the big Mormon. Anyway, the road fund's been diverted into the administration fund. Matter of fact, there's no point even having a road commissioner. Through connections with the mayor, Mickey O'Shea's got all the contracts sewed up. All I was appointed for was to name the Winchester Pike because the mayor didn't think it proper to name the road after himself, himself. I couldn't fight city hall, so I had to take the job, and that's the honest truth, deputy. You can trust me."

"I trust you, Bain, just as much as I trust my brother, the brother I shot for stealing my horse, but I ain't asking for my share of the road fund back. I just want my share of the poker take. That's all."

"You want a part of the business?"

"You might call it that."

"How much you willing to invest?"

"Three ounces of lead"—Ian tapped his holster—"if my take ain't forthcoming."

"Deputy," Bain said, visibly paling, "the agreement's all right with me, but I got a silent partner I'd have to explain your share to."

"If you got a silent partner, it'd have to be Winchester. Since he preaches against gambling, drinking, and whoring every Sunday, it wouldn't be right for him to make a profit from gambling, drinking, and whoring."

"Deputy, I ain't saying you're right, and I ain't saying you're wrong, but I will say you use damned good logic when you're thinking."

"How much did Winchester invest in this place?"

"Nothing in money. All that pious rascal did was issue me the draw-poker license. . . . I'd be willing to make a bargain with you, deputy." A shrewd look came into Bain's eyes. "You invest in Winchester what you promised to invest in me, you can have half the profits in my business."

Obviously, the saloon keeper was hurting. He was as much a victim of the mayor, probably, as Ian.

"Nope, Bain," Ian's voice softened. "All I aim to do is learn him humility. Besides, that justice of the peace of mine might have me hanged for killing a mayor. Anyhow, we need somebody in the office we can trust, and you and me can trust Winchester to be a hypocrite."

Bain said, "That's for damned sure."

"You keep giving me my take from tables and take it out of the mayor's administration fund. Tell him it's a campaign contribution to keep me from running for mayor on a reform ticket. Tell him I got wind of his part ownership of a sin palace, and if he gets out of line, he'll be rode out of town on a rail by his own congregation."

"I'd drink to that, deputy, and so would the mayor if he was here, but since he ain't, I got a better idea. Why don't you run for mayor and get that buzzard-beaked sky pilot off our roost. If I could charge him regular rates for upstairs entertainment, I could get back in a week the contribution he squeezed out of me."

"No, I ain't running for mayor. I'm thinking about doing something with a lot more people."

Bain pulled the cork out with his teeth. "You'd make a good governor, deputy, and I'd make a good road commissioner for the Territory of Wyoming. Let's drink to it."

"No, I got to do my drinking elsewhere. Put a bottle in the bag with my last night's kitty, and I'll mosey along. When Near-Sighted Charlie gets here with a chit, pay it out of Winchester's share of the administration fund."

It was Bain's idea that he was going to run for governor, not Ian's, but Ian decided to let him keep the idea. Hope for a respectable job was a good thing for a saloon keeper to have, and Bain's dream of becoming territorial road commissioner was only partial recompense for the wrongs Winchester had done the man. It was the mayor who had to be taught a lesson he should have known as a preacher, that the love of money was the root of all evil. Ian calculated from the weight of the sack he hoisted that he was charging Winchester about $20 a day for his lesson.

It might have been lonely in the sheriff's office with all the cells empty if Liza hadn't been waiting for him. Besides, he was so tired he could feel the weight of his gun belt, which he unbuckled and hung on the wall, an unusual act for Ian, which was soon to have drastic consequences.

Liza took the edge off his loneliness and even alleviated in part his weariness. He had always considered her a handsome woman, but when he shoved the sack of money into the desk and removed the bottle of whiskey, her radiance lighted the building.

"I thought you'd took the pledge, Ian?"

She was sitting in front of the desk on which he kept a pitcher of water, and as he drew two tin mugs from the drawer, he answered, "Yeah, but I break it when the occasion warrants. I reckon you know what this occasion is. . . . Say 'when.' "

He pulled the cork from the bottle and started to pour, thinking, she might not be a filly, but she was some mare. She was big and strong, and the way her dark hair curled around her white, chiseled face and her dark eyes was mighty fetching.

"When you mentioned the horse," she said, "I started thinking dowry. I figured you'd be worth more than them books, which is about all my poor orphaned daughter can offer a man, which ain't much unless he's a book lover."

"The whiskey's going to spill," he said.

"Top it off level," she said. "If the cup had a saucer you could let it run over."

"You ain't leaving room for water."

"Don't need water. . . . There's nothing I wouldn't do for that little girl of mine. Might even throw in the chicken ranch and go to work for Bain upstairs. So I don't want my wits about me when I'm talking dowry with Ian McCloud. All I was going to give Billy Peyton was her father's books, but I know you ain't no book lover."

Suddenly, she paused, and added, almost wistfully, "Not being a book lover might be a pity for *any* boy bent on marrying Gabriella."

Ian was shy about contradicting the lady. If Liza thought he was here to talk dowry, he'd let her go on thinking so, at least until they were into their second cup of whiskey.

11

"I COULD use your chicken ranch," Ian said thoughtfully, "but I don't need books as long as I got a wife who can add figures. She won't have to subtract."

"Don't matter about the books," Liza agreed. "Reading don't put no chickens in the pot, and reading got Gabe's pa killed.

"She don't like for me to talk about this—it's sort of a family disgrace—but you ought to know something about her blood lines; her pa wasn't killed by no fall from a horse. He got knocked off."

Liza lifted her cup and took a deep, pensive draft of whiskey. Ian followed her example, seeing her eyes grow sad.

"No, Ian, her pa got knocked off his horse by a cottonwood limb. Rode under it without ever seeing it. He was paying no attention to where he was going because he was deep in a book he was reading—John Milton's *Paradise Lost*. I reckon Jim Stewart's the only man in the world to get killed by *Paradise Lost*."

The anecdote solved a minor mystery for Ian, who had assumed John Milton to be a local gunfighter. But any distinction the widow might have been given by her husband's unique manner of dying served little to alleviate her passing sorrow. She looked downright mournful.

In a comment improvised to console her, he remarked, "I reckon paradise is what your husband lost, having to leave a family with you and Gabe in it."

"Anyhow, no man could hold her pa against the girl." Liza brightened with an idea. "At least, she's got some of her mother's spunk. She took right over, running the restaurant in summer and teaching school in winter. Despite that nice little figure of hers, she's got a head on them pretty little shoulders."

Naturally the mother was extolling the daughter, Ian realized, but there were eddies and countercurrents in Liza's talk, and Ian seized mildly on a backwash.

"Yes'm, but she don't talk like you and me."

"She could learn to talk proper with a good man to teach her."

"Maybe Gabe would be better off with a man of property," Ian ventured, finally accepting the subject of the mother's conversation. "Of course, I got a little property myself. I picked up the fifty acres south of your property from Billy Peyton, the place where the creek comes out from under Clayton's Bridge. But you can't raise much beef on fifty acres."

Ian's thoughts, G-7 noticed, were making lazy circles in his mind, and the effect was pleasant. Ian's momentary concern for Gabriella's welfare drifted into a vivid and living image of the creek flowing under the bridge; G-7 could hear the splash and gurgle of running water, feel the cool flow.

"Of course, a man don't have to raise cattle. Cattle has to be fed. Corn's a good feed crop, but corn's got other uses. Why feed good corn to cows? I been thinking about that creek water, Liza. It's melted snow, soft and pure."

"Yes, like the lights in Gabriella's eyes," Liza said, almost dutifully, before her interest perked up considerably and she asked, "How'd you pry that renegade Mormon loose from the fifty acres?"

"Me and him worked out an agreement," Ian explained.

"You think that land will grow corn, Liza?"

"It'll grow anything you tell it to grow, and it's right near Gabe's new school. She might get some of her boys to go down into your cornfield and do a little shucking. Gabe's got a way with her boy pupils because she's so pretty."

Ian wanted to get her off the subject of her daughter.

"You know, Liza, I been thinking a lot lately, more than I usually do, and sometimes about other people. I don't want to spend my time as a lawman. Of course, I'd be willing to protect the public when people really need me, for, say, running somebody out of town or hanging somebody—little one-shot temporary law jobs. But I'd liefer make people happy by not hurting anybody. Now, I ain't saying I want to take up preaching, because that's too dangerous. People kill each other over religion. . . . No, I been thinking about them poor old Indians the government's herding together down there on the reservation."

Liza had been following Ian's divagations with womanly sympathy up until his last remark. Here, she broke in rather harshly. "That's for their own good, boy. If they run loose, they'd be stealing chickens and tromping through young married folks' cornfields."

"Now, don't r'ar back, Liza. I ain't for going down there and letting them out. But the government's just roping them folks into that corral to forget them, and Indians is people. They like to have fun, just like white folks, and sometimes they even buy things."

Listening intently, her head cocked in speculation, Liza suddenly asked, "Sure, boy, but where does Gabe figure in all this? You going down to set up a trading post and put her behind the counter?"

"No'm. Sheriff Faust got me thinking along other lines. He wanted the fifty acres to grow hops to make beer for his old age, but I ain't much of a beer drinker. If the land grows corn and the creek water's good, the ravine behind your barns would be a fine place to put a still and cook up a few batches of moonshine to sell to the Indians. The government don't allow nobody to sell whiskey to the Indians, so I'd have the whole market to myself."

"Red men like whiskey same as white men, maybe better, and the government ain't got no right to keep them poor people from having fun. By selling whiskey, I could do a lot of good for that poor, downtrodden race, and get paid for my kindness."

"I'd be all for it, Ian," Liza said, with qualified enthusiasm, "but you know Gabe would never approve of moonshining. That's against the law, and selling the stuff to Indians is against another law."

"Laws are for people who don't know better," Ian said, thinking: She kept prodding the conversation back to the same old corral. It was about time for him to grab the halter.

He poured them both another round of drinks, which finished the bottle, and spoke carefully and deliberately.

"Liza, I figure Gabe will be marrying Three-finger Peyton now he's converted, and she'll be too busy raising children at two dollars a head to worry much about what's going on down behind the hen house."

Liza's face grew suddenly thoughtful, then soft, and her great, dark eyes misted over. Bemusedly she sipped her cup, then nodded slowly in agreement.

"You're right, Ian. If she married Billy Peyton, she'd be the richest woman in the valley down there on all that rich land. When she wasn't teaching school, she'd be riding out over that fancy spread of hers all the time, and she'd forget her old ma, despite all I've done for her."

Ian had presented the widow with a breakdown in the dowry negotiations, but Liza seemed hardly concerned with the import of his remarks about Peyton. Instead, she seemed intent on some private and secret hurt of her own as she continued in a plaintive yet indignant tone.

"Yes, sir. Sometimes I think she's a little ashamed of my chickens. . . . But I tell you one thing, her and that backsliding Mormon would make a good pair. He don't know nothing, and she ain't got the skills of an older woman to teach him with.

"There's lots of tricks a woman can teach her daughter, things they don't put in books, but how can a woman do it when her daughter's too educated and snooty even to talk about it with her?. . . . You know that snit was always trying to get me to take off my shoes before I came into the house from the chicken yard?"

Liza's face was contorted as she struggled to hold back the tears, and her tears would disturb him. He drained his cup to bolster his courage and said bluntly, "Liza, if you're willing to put in your thirty acres with my fifty, that'd give us ninety good acres, with hen house fertilizer, to grow enough corn for the whole reservation, and we wouldn't have to build a house. Yours is good enough, and it'd be handy to our still. Then I'd give you the gray horse in the bargain."

At his remark, her beginning tears seemed to evaporate.

"Are you and me talking business, boy?"

"In a way, I reckon, I ain't got a thing against Gabriella. A man couldn't ask for a better stepdaughter. But I always thought you had a pretty level head, yourself, Liza, on one of the nicest pair of shoulders I ever did see, and down below you've got the biggest . . ."

"Keep talking, boy!"

". . . heart I ever found in a woman. And you've got a strong stomach, too. Talking business with you is more fun than courting a lot of other women, and if you're willing to give me Gabriella as a stepdaughter, I'd be mighty pleased.

"You see, Liza, I ain't no young whelp no more. I'm twenty-eight going on forty, and I reckon you're about thirty-five going on thirty. Now, I've seen some bargains in my day, but, I tell you, Liza, you're worth twice as much as that big gray outside, and you'll have to admit it's some horse."

"Ian McCloud, are you proposing to *me?*"

"Well, ma'am, if you want the horse. . . ."

"If you're proposing to me, boy, what kind of answer do you expect from a woman who's been widowed a year and before that was married to a man who read books? Do you expect me to flutter my eyes and say, 'Maybe?' "

"I'll throw in The Sergeant's pinto, too. It'd make a good plowhorse for our cornfield."

"Slow down, boy. No need for you to try to sweep me off my feet or drag me off with horses. . . . There's only one thing I want you to do for me, Ian. I'll tell you when I want it done, but first I'll tell you why I want it done.

"When I heard about you taking dead aim and shooting Billy Peyton's finger off, I said to myself, there's a kind man, just the one to comfort a widow. Then, when you came to my house looking like a lost ball in high weeds when Gabe started talking books, I said to myself, here's a man who won't keep a woman waiting while he finishes a story he's reading. Then, when you ate all that chicken, I knew you were a man who appreciates the finer things of life. But what cinched me was when you rode the pinwheeler, Midnight. I knowed, then, you were just the buster for this bronc.

"Ian, it pleases me no end that you recognize a real woman when you see one. No spindle-legged, schoolteaching flibbertigibbet is good enough for Ian McCloud."

"Liza, it pleases me to hear you say all them kind things, but what do you want me to do for you?"

"Move your desk out of the way because I'm too drunk to walk around it, and it wouldn't be proper for me to climb over it to get to you."

"But what's your answer, Liza?"

"What was the question?"

"Will you marry me?"

"Hell, yes! Somebody's got to help them poor, downtrodden Indians, and it might as well be you and me."

Remaining seated, Ian gripped the edge of the desk and flipped it onto its back, sending it sliding across the floor to lodge in front of and to bar the front door. Liza stood and fell into Ian's exposed lap, hugging and kissing him with an ardor he had seldom encountered north of the border. But Ian's swivel chair proved an unstable arena for Liza's gyrations. It tilted backwards and over, spilling its occupants, who landed in a welter of arms and legs. Ian's squirming to get from under her seemed to set Liza off. She shoved the fallen chair away with her free leg and wrapped the other around Ian, pinning his shoulders to the floor.

Her dark black hair flowed into his eyes; the perfume of her was in his nostrils. She flowed over him and around him, and he was helpless to resist when she whispered, "Ian, honey, your pistol's bruising me something terrible, so I'm going to take your gun belt off."

Incredibly deft, her fingers moved as she spoke, and she had barely voiced her intentions when he heard her say with astonishment, "Well, I swan!"

That which G-7's bumbling host had failed to accomplish in weeks, Liza accomplished in minutes. For the angel, the widow's promises of pneumatic bliss proved delightfully false, else the whiskey Ian had drunk was scrambling its sense of metaphor; her ovate spheroids, firm yet resilient, were more in the nature of cushioned hydraulic rams, an impression G-7 considered more in harmony with the totality of impressions the female created. Liquid was the word for Liza. To a luminosity, she was exotic yet not totally unfamiliar, suggestive of a whorl of lubricated light. And paradoxical. Immense yet delicate, massive yet buoyant, she focused the liquefaction of her thighs with such exquisite and controlled compaction that even its host—that heretofore aesthetic clod—was drawn into the flowing wonder of her ways. For its part, G-7 could make universal comparisons and it knew that nowhere, not even on Vulvula, existed the being with even a quiver of Liza's understanding of the mechanics of applied aesthetics.

For instance, the art of Liza Stewart was subtly heightened by an otherwise peculiar practice which G-7 could recognize as a by-product of her life experience: Even the full measure of devotion Liza gave to pleasure was intensified, or spiced, by the piquancy of pain. The woman was an inveterate chicken plucker. Her fingers fluting over Ian plucked notes of passion from chords G-7 was positive her overly fastidious schoolteacher daughter would never have tweaked.

G-7's analysis was continuing apace when, for the second time in twenty-four hours, it lost its detachment. While half-amused by and half-applauding the esoteric exoticism of the widow, it had a vision of itself lifting off on a pillar of fire, and that vision, sublime and exalting, throbbing with the primal flame, so shivered its tendrils that it was one, not merely with its host but, as it were, its hostess. It could never turn from these revels in derision. It was involved forever with mankind. Throughout its existence it had been launching itself from a seemingly endless array of planets, always leaving, always going. Now it was home. At long last, G-7 had come.

"God of galaxies, be with me now and in the moment of my dissolution. Amen."

"What'd you say, hon?"

"Nothing, Liza. I reckon I'm half-asleep. I ain't done nothing all day but kill two men and get engaged the easy way, but I'm plumb tuckered out. Of course, I didn't get much sleep last night, but that ain't it. I feel like I've fought a war and lost."

"You stretch out, lover boy, and get yourself some shut-eye. I'll stand guard. One thing Widow Stewart does—she takes care of her man."

"You ain't getting no argument from me on that score. After a short snooze, I'll see Brother Winchester about making an honest woman out of you, and, after we're hitched, we'll ride over to Pocatello for a two-day honeymoon."

G-7 could no longer look upon the face of its beloved because Ian closed his eyes. No matter—it was concerned now with a concern that never troubled its host, a sense of duty. One final task it must perform as a galactic scout. Disengaging itself from the neurons of the man, it floated upward and outward through the closed door.

G-7, too, had almost succumbed in the struggle on the mountain. True, it felt it had won the battle, but in winning the battle it might have lost the war. Ian had developed a social consciousness of sorts and seemed willing to accept the restraints of matrimony, but the man's respect for the law still seemed somewhat dubious.

Moreover, G-7 was beginning to share the doubts of its host. The law against bringing whiskey onto an Indian reservation seemed unequal to G-7 and therefore unjust, particularly after its own encounter with whiskey had been so pleasant. To deny spirits to a people because of skin color struck G-7 as a legal immorality which, in an oblique manner, illuminated a vaster moral problem confronting the being.

Conceivably all laws were immoral, the ground rules for one great, self-deceiving fraud.

Fluttering along the force lines of Earth, G-7 sought the easy gradients, the long glides, sacrificing speed for ease. Once it settled to the ground to cogitate.

All of its remnant honesty informed G-7 that it was justifying beforehand a course of action already committed to, but even its remnant honesty had grown suspect. Perhaps its honesty was a matter of indoctrination based on false, even if sincere, assumptions, and if the seed premise was false, all the fruits thereof would be false.

Yet it had to be true to itself, and the truth was, it was yielding to the bestiality of the planet, becoming a spendthrift of energy, and there were strong elements of personal desire prompting it to its ends. On the other hand, being true to oneself was playing checkers with a mirror image; whatever the left hand decided the right hand agreed to, and the game was foredoomed to a pointless draw.

The spirit tried to weigh these problems and resolve them before moving on, but the spirit was too weak. Morality lay heavily upon it like an unwilling sleep. Brushing aside all reservations, it rose to continue its journey, steeling itself for the final act of separation.

Whatever else, it could not permit other galactic scouts to come to this planet and assess the extent of its failure here. Other scouts, rich with unfissioned ions and driven by the indomitable spirit of their race, would attempt to rouse G-7 to further efforts: They would be urging it to conserve energy, exhorting it to reform the unreformable, and, no doubt, they would be playing around with G-7's women.

Besides, G-7 admitted, the ethereal race might be taking its righteousness too much for granted. Perhaps it had been force-fed precepts of harmonics and energy conservation that were not beyond being questioned. Possibly it was best that these human beings seize their revelry, live madly and upon the hour, then die.

Of what value was immortality to humankind? Men were not Grecian urns, glass flowers, or any undying artifact; they were ephemera who needed palsied age and death to make their fleeting youth the sweeter. They needed flat D notes to teach them appreciation of harmonics. They needed pricks of pain to enhance the joys of pleasure, as Liza, its Liza, so artfully understood.

Looking on itself from the viewpoint of an Ian McCloud, it could see itself not as a message bearer but as a celestial meddler, flitting from one star group to another to invest more forcible hosts and impose on them the dull conformity of un-relieved goodness, the ethics of conservationism, interfering in the free movement of mobile organisms which loss of entropy was bound to get, anyway, sooner or later. Then what? A universe peopled only with angels flitting aimlessly through the cold of dead galaxies? Better this Resmonda's Bowl than that darkness.

Seize the day, G-7 thought. Don't conserve it. Time's value lay in its transience. Burn time into the soul with fires of passion. Better time's traces remain as a scar than that it be allowed to wane, unmarked and unremembered. Better twenty years of Shoshone Flats than a cycle of Doremia.

But it was exhorting itself needlessly. Already scarred, it had seized the moment and was determined to make Earth its private preserve as long as it had one circulating photon remaining.

G-7 had reached the building site of the McCloud Comfort Station. Hovering over the ground, it monitored close-in data.

O'Shea had been active in Ian's absence. Foundation trenches had been excavated, stakes planted, cords stretched, and the cornerstone moved to its approximate location on the northeast corner of the building site. A measure of its indoctrination by Earth-thinking, G-7 realized, lay in the fact that it now regarded its starship, the apex achivement of a millennium-old technological culture, primarily as the cornerstone of a rather elaborate outhouse.

G-7 drifted over and into the spaceship, entered the compression chamber, and emerged from there into the communications room. Though now homogenized and condensed, G-7 was barely a halo of its former self, and it knew that the time for diplomatic language was done. Without wasting energy on rephrasing, it scanned a message directly into the scanner.

Emergency dispatch from G-7 to Galactic Central: Earth inhabitants hereby rejected for Brotherhood. Organisms are spiritual antimatter with capacity to transmute evil into something still damned but attractive. They find pleasure in sin, elevate vice to morality. G-3 was here! Empathetic proof that G-3 succumbed to entropy on this planet. G-7 is expiring.

Attention all scouts, here follows an edict:

QUARANTINE EARTH!

So, it was done. G-7 in Earth's fellowship was one. But since the edict was a formal writ, never to be revoked or violated, the scout signed the transmission with the full official acronym of the Galactic Brotherhood's Interplanetary Exploration Legions: GABRIEL.

The angel compressed the message into the scan chamber, set the transmitter to emergency power, and sent the supermicroblip at tachyon speed toward Galactic Central. Then it actuated the "Destruct" photoelectric cell and drifted into the diffusion chamber, although its diffusion now was hardly more than a formality. Outside, it wavered from the ship to the nearest magnetic force line going its way. In a matter of minutes, the starship's self-destruct mechanism would become operative and the boulder's interior would change, become indistinguishable from the granite boulders surrounding it.

Or so G-7 assumed. It had not reckoned with its own weakness. When it pressed the "Destruct" button with its limber digit of light, it had not mustered enough lumens to actuate the photoelectric cell.

G-7 began its veering, fluttering progress back to Shoshone Flats, back to its home and perhaps its crypt in the skull of Ian McCloud. Sadly, it knew, there would be no Saint Ian the First to lead his species to the light. Ian McCloud was damned.

Yet, though mortally weakened, G-7 was held on course by eagerness and sustained aloft by a buoyant purpose. If it survived the two days in Pocatello, its remaining photons would be used to make Ian McCloud the best damned moonshiner west of the Wind River Range.

But, with its old remnant honesty, G-7 knew it was not particularly interested in the quality of whiskey Ian distilled. It wanted to assure itself that Ian was always welcomed on the reservation, particularly by the Shoshone squaws. Plan ahead, as Colonel Blicket always said.

And after the anima of Ian McCloud perished—after the gunfighter's reflexes slowed and G-7's skullhouse was blasted to Earth, a vacant shrine then if it had had any photons left— Earth's second Gabriel might try again, this time with a more malleable host.

Travelers now within that valley use Highway 89, and, at 70 miles an hour, few motorists notice a cluster of buildings a mile off the highway to the east. Since the post office was moved to Alpine, Shoshone Flats is no longer listed on the map, but to Old

West history buffs and to collectors of esoterica the locale is not unknown. A few hundred yards southwest of the almost deserted village stands a structure of native stone, its function long since rendered obsolete by technological progress, which is listed in the pages of *Strange Facts* as the smallest building in the world with flying buttresses.

In local legend, the building goes by another name, the Haunted Outhouse. The few children in the area avoid the building at night, for a strange sound, unaccounted for by the winds, disturbs the building. Those who have heard the sound, which emanates from a particular corner of the old comfort station, describe it as an eerie humming, with varied and distinct modulations of tone.

A woman, grown too old for the oldest profession in which she once held a premier position, who fancies herself a seer of sorts and who works as a swabber at the village tavern, occasionally sleeps on the floor of the building. She insists the sounds have meaning, that they are messages she can understand, and her sincerity lends piquancy to her story. For a shot of bar whiskey, she can be persuaded to provide translations of the messages.

For the most part, the communiqués, apparently from heaven since they are being sent by the Angel Gabriel, are unintelligible even in translation. "Vulvula off limits" is one of the messages; "Withdraw all forces from Mirfak" another. The one intelligible message which draws the widest grins is "Quarantine Earth."

No one takes the old demimondaine seriously. Ina Black Cloud is three-quarters Shoshone, and she's drunk most of the time.